DANGEROUS CURVES AHEAD

WATCHERS CREW BOOK 3

INES JOHNSON

THOSE JOHNSON GIRLS

ONE

The tapping of raindrops on the window was intermittent; sometimes a steady pitter-patter, then in the next minute, a reluctant deluge. The thick droplets dried up immediately after impact when they hit the glass pane. The disappearing act was likely due to the brilliant sun shining above.

It was the kind of day my grandfather would've called God weeping for mankind. It was the kind of day my father would've called God pissing on mankind. In my opinion it was a great day.

The winter was over. I was out of the knits and sweaters that added bulk to my curvy frame. Today, I was in one of my favorite sundresses. Sundresses allowed me to come out of my shell and show off my best assets; my calves and shoulders. Though most of the time, the male gaze stayed focused on the double D's on my chest.

I sat in a pretty floral dress, my wedged heels crossed at my ankles. My toenails were done in a fun design that matched my fingernails, which also matched the ribbon I'd tied in my hair, which also complimented the floral earrings dangling from my lobes. Because I was never comfortable showing too much skin, I may have been prone to over-accessorizing.

I wasn't a flashy person. Though I did often use my clothing to reflect my mood. And today, I felt a rainbow of optimism on the horizon.

Also on the horizon, across the street in an office building, I spied a man in a business suit and a woman in a blouse and skirt making out. The man had the woman pressed up against the closed door. My eyes widened as his hands went up her shirt.

From this distance, I saw the divot of her belly button. I'd seen any number of belly buttons in my lifetime; on the beach, in the girl's locker room, walking down the street on a Saturday night. But in this context, there was something wicked about it.

I wasn't wicked. I was a good girl. But I couldn't look away.

The man's palm traveled under her blouse up

higher and higher on her torso. My eyes kept in step with his fingers. My hand clutched at my chest at the sight of her bra; lacy and fire-engine red. He pulled the bra cup down and exposed her nipple. The contrast to the red lace and the pink areola was stark.

A crack of thunder split the air, darkening the skies and scattering the raindrops. The two broke apart. They looked out the window, up at the darkening sky. At the same time, I jumped in my seat. I averted my gaze, doubtful they saw me.

I pressed a hand to my cheeks to feel them flaming. Then reached down to finger the rosary beads at my heart. The texture of the beads calmed me. When I looked up, the couple was gone. The office was empty.

I took a deep breath and turned from the window. Glancing up at the utilitarian wall clock, I noted that my appointment should've started fifteen minutes ago.

My fifth book in Hera Publishing's inspirational romance line had just reached into the top 10,000 on Amazon. There were over a million books available for sale at the online retailer. That was a big deal for an inspirational author like me who ended each book with the hero and heroine approaching first base. It proved that readers wanted more of my self-assured heroines who met their heroes inside church groups instead of the stepbrother down the hall or the were-wolf who threw her over his shoulder.

My first series, *Righteous Calling*, was comprised of twenty-something, career women who returned to their small towns, and then back to their roots in church, to reconnect with their Creator. Along the way, they each found love amidst the pews. I sat in my editor's office waiting to pitch my next series.

The series I hoped to write next was called *Tender Kisses*. For this series, I planned to go with the tide of the market and write new adult characters. These love stories would be about Christians meeting at Bible college. I was also debating pitching a future series called *Love's Calling* about missionaries finding romance while abroad.

I wasn't making a killing selling sweet romances, but they paid the bills. It was enough so that I didn't have to rely on my parents for money. My mother would love nothing more than to have me back home. That was the last thing I wanted; being the buffer in my parents' marriage. *Til death do us part* was less a vow and more a threat in my parents' case.

The pitter-patter of the rain died down, and I heard the striking of heels across the floor. Moira Young walked into her office in fire-red stilettos and a black designer pantsuit that fit her size six waist like a glove. Her face looked professionally made up as though she'd walked off a high-fashion shoot. Her lip-gloss was perfect for her dark skin tone. She could've been Tyra Banks's more attractive sister. Sitting in my flower dress and hair bows, I felt like anything but *America's Next Top Model*.

I sucked in my size twelve gut which caused my double D's to rise. I'd managed eyeliner and gloss, but that was the extent of my makeup collection. Most of my advance and royalties went to my closet, which I used to hide my chubby flaws.

Moira had taken over the publishing house after my third book had been published. My last editor had left, gone off to a big New York publishing house. She'd taken a few authors with her. I hadn't been included.

That was fine. I was loyal to Hera Publishing. This company had given me my first break. I planned to stay with them for the long haul.

"All right, Mary Kate."

I forced a smile. I hated when people truncated

my name. But I wanted to start this meeting off on a positive note.

Moira looked up at me with a thousand-watt smile that didn't reach her smoke-lined eyes.

"I'm excited to talk about your future with the company," she said in an even tone.

Her even tone didn't alarm me. Moira never spoke in exclamation points. Only periods and semi-colons.

I, on the other hand, was prone to exclaim. "I'm excited, too!"

"We're making some changes," Moira continued, glazing over my expression. "You're a valued author for Hera Publishing. You have a loyal, but small following."

My following wasn't small. Had she not read the latest author report? I wasn't exactly one in a million, but 10,000 wasn't half bad.

"I think it could be bigger," Moira said. "We want to take you in a new direction."

Perfect. I opened my mouth to pitch my *Tender Kisses* and *Love's Calling* series.

Before I could, Moira continued. "We want you to add steam."

Steam? As in steam punk? I had no clue about that genre. It also had no place in inspirational and sweet romance. It was more in the realm of science fiction and fantasy romance.

When Moira came onboard, Hera introduced a few new lines. The Athena line, for paranormal, science fiction, and fantasy romance. The Dione line, for contemporary. And the Aphrodite line, for erotica. With my current sales, I felt fairly secure that my career would continue at the Demeter line, for the sweeter side of romance. Was she asking me to write for the Athena line?

"Many Christian authors, inspirational authors, and sweet authors are opening the doors during their love scenes," Moira said. "There's even Amish erotica."

So I'd heard. I wasn't Amish. I'd been raised in a traditional Christian household. The kind where the parents stop going to church after the kids outgrew their fancy Easter clothes.

"Your readers are buying it," Moira said.

I frowned, having lost the train of conversation. "It?"

Moira paused and blinked at me as though she remembered I was there while she gave her monologue. "Sex. Your readers are buying books with sex in them."

I wanted to disagree. I wanted to insist that my

readers were girls just like me. Good girls, who sat with their legs crossed, and went to church every Sunday.

Well, I didn't go to church every Sunday. In fact, I hadn't been since... last Easter? I think?

"If you want to keep writing for us, Mary Kate, you're going to have to pop your heroines' cherries."

This time it was me who paused and blinked. I shook my head like I used to shake the bunny ear antennas on my grandparents' old television. There had to be something wrong with the reception.

"You can keep the story lines in your wheel house," Moira said. "I'd love to see a good girl go on a sexual journey of discovery with a bad boy in need of redemption. I'll need to see an outline and the first three chapters by the end of the month."

An outline? I hadn't been required to submit an outline since my first book. Not only was I being asked to write something completely out of my depth, I was being treated like a new author.

"And what if I don't want to add steam or open doors in my stories?" I asked.

Moira frowned as though she hadn't considered the query. "You can always buy out your existing contract. But you still owe us two more books."

I didn't have the money lying around to buy out

of two books. I was budgeted down to the penny. I opened my mouth to bargain, but Moira's phone rang. She picked up the receiver. I was effectively dismissed.

I rose, preparing to leave the office. I cast a glance out the window. On the bright side, the sky had cleared, taking the rain away. Off in the distance, I spied the multicolored stripes of a rainbow. I was just on the wrong end of the arch.

TWO

By the time I stepped out of Hera Publishing's office, the rainbow showed bright across the sky. Unfortunately, it did not brighten my mood. I walked over to my car; a Chevy Buick. Not one of the newer models in the young hipster commercials. It was a 1970's model. I'd gotten it from my grandfather. He'd named the car Lucille because she had the devil in her.

I sat back in Lucille's plush seat and closed my eyes. What was I going to do? It's not like I was a literary author out for awards for my craft.

I wrote romance novels.

A lot of people looked down on the genre. In my four years of writing in the industry, I'd met so many women who were feeding their families with the money they garnered from writing what the general public called bodice rippers, chick lit, and mommy porn.

I didn't turn my nose up at steamy romance. It just wasn't my thing. But it would have to become my thing if I wanted to keep making a living.

So, what were my options?

I could quit. Take my work to another publisher. Hope that my audience followed me. But I could be sued for breach because I owed the publisher more books.

Or, I could give them what they wanted. Sex.

I turned the ignition over. Lucille groaned, shuddered, and stalled.

Two race cars sped down the street, engines roaring, exhaust polluting the air. It was an increasing problem in the city, just like teenage pregnancy in high schools, the spread of STDs in elder communities, and the rate of divorce in mature communities. People were all moving too fast.

Twenty minutes later, I pulled up to my parents' pristine house. The lawn was recently manicured. The shutters had a fresh coat of paint. There were bright flowers blooming in the window box.

Inside, my sister's kids were wreaking havoc in

the family room. Louisa Mae had four children under the age of six. She greeted me belly first with number five. Her thick brown tresses were coiled in an elaborate knot on top her head, not a hair out of place. Eye shadow highlighted her green eyes, and a thin sheen of lip-gloss accented her full lips.

We had the exact same facial features, but that's where it ended. Even though she was five months pregnant, she carried her baby weight well. Her figure still held its hourglass. Any weight she'd gained belonged to the baby in her belly and didn't dare touch anywhere else on her body.

"You're late," Louisa Mae said. "I've been playing referee with the parents for the last hour."

"Mommy," said one of her boys. Honestly, I couldn't tell if he was Walter or Brandon. They looked exactly alike except for an inch or two. "He hit me!"

"Go give him a hug and show him that in this family we love," was my sister's response.

The kid pouted off, unsatisfied. I doubted a hug was on the horizon.

"Are they fighting?" I said, indicating my head towards the kitchen where I saw my mom moving about.

"You know they never fight. They barely talk,"

said my sister. "It's a cold front."

I looked around the living room. "Where's your husband?"

"Business trip." Louisa Mae struggled with a diaper bag. There were bags under her eyes that would never blend into her eye shadow. "He just got a new account and has to be available to his clients at all times."

Charles, Louisa Mae's husband, was some corporate bigwig. I wasn't sure exactly what he did? Mainly because I had never had a full conversation with the man in the seven years he'd been my brother-in-law. He wasn't around the family much, but he was always available to his clients.

My two-year-old niece, who was dressed as a pink fairy with wings, was throwing a tantrum over her cartoon program ending. Louisa Mae tried to explain that mommies couldn't make the television network play the episode again. The two eldest boys weren't hugging; they were shoving at each other behind their mother's back. The one-year-old sat quietly on the sofa watching it all go down. I couldn't tell if he was taking notes or wishing he were somewhere else.

My sister found another program for the fairy princess and then separated the two eldest boys. "What took you so long to get here?" she said to me.

"Meeting at my publisher's," I said from my post in the doorway. "My editor wanted to discuss some upcoming projects."

My sister frowned. "You're still writing those smutty stories?"

I felt like throwing a tantrum myself. Maybe that would get my sister to change the channel away from this repeated argument. "They want to take my books in a new direction. They really believe in my talent."

It wasn't exactly a lie. Moira said she believed in my talent. She just wanted me to take my talent in an area where I was uncomfortable treading.

"I don't know how you'll ever find a husband with a hobby like that," Louisa Mae said as she arched her back with a grimace. "Aren't most romance writers women? Plus you're going to keep packing it on if you sit around all day typing on keyboards. You might as well become a secretary. At least that way you could try to snag your boss or a junior executive."

Louisa Mae walked into the fray of her children,

who were now bickering over the remote control, before I could mount a counteroffensive. The only reason my sister went to college was to get her MRS degree. When that didn't work, she got a job as an Executive Assistant and that's where she met Charles Rasmussen. There was already a Mrs. Rasmussen, but Charles had insisted they were separated. Luckily, he was divorced before Walter, or was it Brandon, had been born. But it wasn't something we talked about.

I left my sister to her family and turned to the matriarch of our own.

"Ah, there you are, Mary Katherine."

Pricilla Elizabeth Wallace straightened, pulling a roast out of the oven. She was dressed in a tailored skirt and blouse, looking every bit the Economics Professor she was. My mother was in her early fifties, but she could easily be mistaken for her late thirties. When we were out together, which wasn't often, we were mistaken for sisters.

"How was your writing club meeting?"

"It was fine, mom. Thanks for asking." I didn't bother to correct her. It was fruitless.

Because our mother was a professor, we always had the expectation of getting higher education degrees. My sister studied Art History, so she could be witty at company parties. I'd minored in Literature and majored in Secondary Education my first year in college.

The Education degree wasn't my idea. It was the only way my mother would pay for such a frivolous minor. She wanted to be sure I had an actual career opportunity on the horizon if my first intention wasn't to find a husband to support me. That career opportunity was teaching. I'd submitted my sweet romance stories in my sophomore year. By my junior year, I had enough money from my first advance to pay for the extra credits for a double major.

My mother placed the roast on the stovetop. She turned and frowned. "Oh Mary Katherine, I wish you'd dressed for dinner."

I looked down at myself. My floral sundress was fine for a business meeting. I thought it was all right for a family dinner. That is, if this was just a family dinner.

"Why?" I looked down the hallway to the front door. "It's just us, right?"

Mom didn't meet my eyes "Where's your father? I asked him to bring in an extra chair. I swear the man is useless. I even wrote it down for him."

"Mom? Why would we need an extra chair if it's just us four at the adult table?"

"And I'm sure you'll only want one helping of the roast." My mother glanced at my Spanx-addled midsection, pretending not to hear me.

I knew she was pretending because she had the same crinkle in her eye she got when my father spoke to her.

"Kurt," she called.

"You don't have to yell, Priscilla." My dad entered the kitchen. Unlike my mother, my father looked his age. The years hadn't been kind to him and he had developed a bit of a beer belly along with a streak of gray in his brown hair. But he was still very handsome.

"I'm right here," he said.

"You weren't right here," insisted my mother. "That's why I had to yell. You didn't bring the extra chair."

"Extra chair for who?" My dad turned and saw me. His face lit up as though he saw a small spot of shade in the glaring sun. "Hello, Mary Katherine."

Dad leaned in and bussed me on the cheek. Mixed in with his cologne was a floral scent I knew wasn't my mother's brand of perfume. Pulling away, I caught a shade of lipstick on his collar that didn't match my mother's skin tone.

"Hey, Daddy." I smiled and kept my mouth shut. It wasn't something we talked about.

My father had been out of work for two years now. Before that my mom had quickly surpassed him as breadwinner. Before I went to college, I'd noticed that the extra set of guest sheets were often missing from the linen closet. I once found them in my sister's old room. I don't know the last time my parents slept in the same bedroom. Or the last time they'd shown any affection towards each other. My writing got me out of the house and out from under my mom's thumb. Dad wasn't so lucky.

"Kurt, will you please get an extra chair?" My mother's tone was a pitch perfect match to my sister's who I could hear scolding one of the boys in the other room.

My father scowled, but turned and did as he was told.

"Who's coming to dinner, Mom?"

"Did I not tell you? The local high school is looking for an English teacher?"

"I met the principal at the school board meeting," said my sister coming into the kitchen. "He's young and handsome."

"And single," said my mom.

Dad came back into the kitchen with the extra chair.

My mother pointed to indicate where my father should set the chair; right next to my usual spot at the dinner table. "So when he gets here, Mary Katherine, don't talk about those little romance stories you write. We wouldn't want him to think you'd be teaching the kids trashy writing."

I stared at the chair that my father unfolded and placed next to my spot. I looked over at my mother, who was carving a thin slice of roast that had my name on it. I glanced at my sister who rubbed her belly absentmindedly with her left hand until her wedding band snagged the fabric of her dress. I looked back at my father who glared at my mother behind her back as he shoved the guest chair up to the table.

I saw the bars at the back of the chair; the unbendable, cold, steel bars. My feet moved towards the front door of their own accord. "I can't stay."

"But it's family night," said my dad. His hand reached out toward me as though I were a puffy cloud taking away his moment in the shade.

"I have a deadline for one of those trashy stories," I said. "It's on my brain and since Mom doesn't want me to talk about it in front of your guest..."

I didn't bother to finish the sentence. I made a beeline for the front door. Then I ran until I got to Lucille. She started on the first try. We tore out of there -speed limit be damned. When I got home, I knew my only choice would be to open up some doors and let out some steam.

THREE

A few days later, my hands still shook from signing the new publishing contract. I stood to make more money for the first steamy book than I made in my last three, sweet books combined. I'd spent the last few days researching the erotic romance industry. A lot of paperback books were tossed across my apartment in disgust. I couldn't believe that modern, thinking, autonomous women were truly into these things.

Billionaires. Stepbrothers. Pseudo-incest. Spanking?

I was trying to get away from my family. Not pull them into my bedroom!

By the end of the week, I still had no clue how I would turn my sweet, virginal heroines into wanton, sexpots that shook their naughty booties at their new daddies or brothers by marriage.

I was already on plan D when I pulled up to a storefront on the other side of town. It did not look like a sex shop. It looked like a boutique sandwiched between a beauty supply store and an electronics store. Across the street was a Babies R Us.

I'd been sitting in my car watching people go in and out of the front doors of Adonis' Novelties. They were a mixed crowd. Mostly middle-aged couples or women of an undeterminable age. It couldn't have been a den of heathens if mature people went in. I just hadn't seen anyone come back out yet.

The website for Adonis' Novelties said they held classes and sold educational and sexual health products. That's why I was here.

I couldn't get past the first few chapters of the best-selling, steamy romance books. I'd tried watching porn online and never got past the first five minutes of any scene. It was so clear that the women in these grainy videos were 'working' and not enjoying the benefits. They kept swiping their hair out of the way of the camera lens. Their heavily made-up faces kept checking for the placement of the camera, paying more attention to it than their coworkers. And their moaning and dirty talking had me hitting the mute button. I didn't know what an orgasm felt like, having never had one myself, but it was clear that their show of passion was all faked.

So, I was here at this adult boutique shop that promised art porn for women by women. I just needed to go in there and get what I needed in order to do my job and keep my independent lifestyle.

I got out of the comfort of Lucille and crossed the parking lot. No sooner did I step onto the sidewalk did two cars zoom up, motors growling. Wheels screeched in protest and smoke rose from beneath the tires. The drivers did a turn I'd only seen in the movies and slid perfectly into the parking lines, landing side by side.

Inside the vehicles, two young men laughed as they shouted at each other through open windows. In the car closer to me was a black man with dark shades that hid his eyes. Even with the shades, I could tell he was looking at me. Through to his passenger window, I saw a blond man. He wore no sunglasses and his smiling, blue eyes pierced my soul. The mischief in them made a giggle bubble in my chest. The heat in them had me pressing my thighs together and ducking my head as my cheeks prepared to blush.

The blond cut his engine and got out. The dark-skinned man held up his middle finger. The blond continued laughing as he crossed the street.

The dark-skinned man turned his gaze back to me. His head dipped, allowing me to see his eyes behind the shades. He scanned my body with a curl to his lip that made me gulp. Men rarely looked at me like that. I felt the heat pouring off of him as he sucked in his lower lip. He dipped his shades down lower, so I saw the intention in his eyes. He winked at me before pulling off in a roar of engines.

When I looked up, the blond was checking me out. His eyes fastened to my breasts. I crossed my arms over my chest. That's when he met my eyes. His were unapologetic and crystal blue. Fathomless blue, like seeing down into the ocean. Only it went on forever and ever.

"Are you headed in?"

I gasped in a lungful of air as his voice brought me back to the surface. I looked at the storefront door. My cheeks blazed red. My mouth wouldn't work to deny my intended destination.

He opened the door for me. Then, to my horror, he followed me inside. He was obviously a creep. I turned to confront him, but he moved past me and headed to the back of the store, then down a hall that looked private.

I turned away from his retreating figure to the sounds of moaning on the other side of the wall. There was a small classroom in the corner of the storefront. The door was open.

Inside, I saw couples; men and women, women paired with women, men paired with men. In each pairing, one partner lay on the floor on a set of cushions. The other partner sat next to them. The partners who lay on the floor had beautiful woven blankets covering their midsections. Their legs lay straight out and their arms were above their heads or out in a T.

It reminded me of the Crucifixion. Though not a single person looked distressed. Everyone's eyes were closed as they all moaned deeply, gutturally, like a chant. My eye caught the sign on the door. Orgasmic Meditation, it read.

My eyes bulged out of my head. I turned back to the people spread out on the pillow-littered floor. They were all fully clothed. No one was touching anyone else.

Was this a way to achieve an orgasm? Just through deep breathing and groaning? They sounded exactly like the women in the online porn videos. But no one was fussing with their hair, or looking around for a camera.

My eyes fell to the person leading the chant. He was older, with a white beard and a gentle smile that reminded me of the preacher at my grandparents' church. My ears turned back to the chanting which called to mind the hymns we used to sing on Sunday mornings. There had been such a feeling of community and love and devotion sitting in the pews.

With the chanting filling my ears, I felt weightless. My spirit felt lulled to enter the room, to join in on the praise song. But then the partners, who were all kneeling, reached beneath the blankets. I couldn't see anything but the movements of their hands beneath the covers. Were they touching...? They couldn't be. Could they?

"Can I help you?"

My body jerked as I turned to see a woman who looked like she'd stepped out of the 60's flower child movement. She could've easily been my mother's contemporary with her white blonde hair, deep blue eyes, and smooth skin. But this woman's look was effortless, natural. Not forced and controlled like my mother's.

"What are you looking for, my dear?" she asked. "Wait, let me guess?"

My throat seized as I watched and waited for her to make up her mind about me and my proclivities. What if she took me to the dildos on the opposite side of the store? Or over to the lesbian video collection in the corner?

"You're here for the Candida movies," she said after a brief pause. "Am I right? I pulled them aside for you."

"Thank you," I breathed in relief.

Candida Royalle was the maker of women-centered, art porn that promised authentic portrayals of love-making and sensuality.

"You should also check out her book, *How to Tell a Naked Man What to Do*. It teaches women to take control of their own sex life. It's perfect if you're having trouble getting your partner to please you."

"Oh, no. It's not for me. I mean it is, but not in that way. You see, I'm a writer."

"Ah, for research then?" She guided me to the cash register and began the process of ringing me up. "Is your new book fiction or nonfiction?"

I hesitated. But this woman was not my mother. She seemed interested in what I was doing for a living. Definitely not my mother.

"Fiction," I said. "I've been writing sweet

romance novels, but my publisher wants me to add steam and open doors to the love scenes."

The woman nodded sagely as she handed back my credit card. "Writing sex is not as easy as insert tab A into slot B. It's about emotion and feeling and communication."

Emotion and feeling, I understood. It was the tabs into slots I was utterly clueless about. Not utterly. I knew what went where. I just didn't know how to describe them with the emotion and feeling of the act. Everything I'd seen had been faked. But these videos I was purchasing were supposed to be the real deal, full of emotion and feeling. The closest thing to voyeurism without being in physical attendance.

She handed the package to me and leaned over the counter as though our business dealing was not yet over. "You know, I was just having this conversation with my -Christopher, come here for a second."

I turned and saw the blond speedster carrying a box of what looked like large pacifiers. He got closer, his eyes lighting on me. When he came up beside me, I saw the label on the box. It read; Anal Plugs.

FOUR

"Christopher," said the older woman. "This is... I'm sorry, dear. I didn't get your name?"

I hadn't left my name when I'd called in earlier. I'd just said I'd be by to pick up the items. Staring into Christopher's fathomless, blue eyes again, I lost my sense. Something inside told me to tell him everything. And so I did.

"Mary Katherine. Mary Katherine Wallace."

"That's a lovely name. I'm Holly and this is Christopher. Christopher, Ms. Wallace here is an author. She's doing research for her novel."

I expected the guy to blanch at the idea of talking about books. Instead, his blue eyes lit up. I had to brace myself by leaning into the counter from the impact. I was an absolute sucker for handsome men. It didn't cause me much trouble. I so rarely spoke to drop dead gorgeous model types.

Christopher gave me his full attention. And then he spoke to me. "Anything I would know?" he asked.

I wrestled to untie my tongue. "I doubt it. Unless you read romance novels?"

"Read them? I inhaled Harlequins as a teenaged boy. The chance to get inside a girl's head? Why would I pass up that opportunity?"

I couldn't tell if he was joking or not? His tone was serious, but mischief clouded those blue of his eyes. Then his face sobered. The mischief fled his gaze and an intelligent front moved in.

"But I have complaints," he said. "A lot of those books set women up for unrealistic expectations."

He sat the box of anal plugs on the counter. Then he motioned me towards a table with chairs. He preceded me and pulled out a chair, looking up at me expectantly.

I was too shocked to do anything but follow.

"Take for example the grand gesture," he continued once we both were seated. "It's the guy that's always in the wrong and has to make an apology speech. But both the guy and the girl have a part in the problem, or the misunderstanding. Then there's the happily-ever-after. The book ends just when everything's getting started, when we all know for a fact that every couple has their ups and downs, and many relationships don't last the first year. My parents have been together for thirty years. They fuss and they fight, but my dad says he wakes up every morning and reaches for my mother, even when he's mad at her."

My toes curled up into the clouds. My ovaries had heart palpitations. On the other side of the wall, I heard the Orgasmic Meditation group. Their chants were no longer in synch. They were also no longer in harmony. Some cries rang higher, others lower.

"But my biggest gripe," Christopher continued his sermon over the chorus of guttural praises in the next room, "is the simultaneous orgasm. Do you know how hard that is to achieve? And not all women are multi-orgasmic. But they expect the guy to do all the work, and all she has to do is lay there. That's what romance novels teach women."

The bell ringing over the entry door broke up the chanting and his speech. Two women entered the shop.

They were both tall with legs for days. The first was pancake thin in a low-cut blouse and hip-hugging skirt. The second was shaped like a soda bottle with a slim torso and then a flaring backside that couldn't be real. But as I looked closer at their faces, I realized that they had to be twins.

"Hi, Ms. Holly," they said in unison.

"Hello, girls," said Holly with a welcoming smile. "Your order came in this morning. I'll grab it for you." She disappeared down the private hall.

"Hey, Crow," purred Soda Bottle. "I hear your crew is having a party tonight."

"We're coming over," said Pancake. "You wanna come to our place for some pre-party fun?"

"Thanks ladies, but no. I'm talking to my new friend, MK."

Pancake and Soda Bottle glanced at me. Holly came out of the back with a package in her hands and motioned the girls over to the cash register. They went without a huff. By the time I turned back around, Christopher, or was it Crow, had his eyes back on me.

"So, tell me about your story, MK."

I looked between the twins and him. They looked like the type of women who knew how to tell a naked man what to do. I'd never even seen a naked man in real life. This, sitting across a table from Christopher, was the closest I'd been to a man in months. "You should probably go with them."

"I'll hook up with them later," he said.

"You could probably get lucky with them. You should know that's not going to happen with me."

The mischief returned to his blue eyes. "I wasn't aware that I'd offered sex. I thought we were having a conversation."

The tips of my ears burned bright red. Of course he wasn't interested in me. Not when he had twin models throwing themselves at him. "I'm sorry. I realize I'm not your type-"

"No," he chuckled. "You're exactly my type, MK."

I liked my name. I thought it made me unique having two first names. Being called two letters by this man with an angelic face and the devil in his eyes, made me feel like a different version of myself. Someone hip and cool.

I shook myself out of it. Inside, I was the same old Mary Katherine. "I'm a virgin."

That should do it. When I laid that bit of knowledge on the men I dated that got them leaning back in their chairs and raising their hand for the check. Christopher leaned back in his chair, but his hand didn't rise to call forth the end of our time together. The look on his face began as a grimace, but it kept spreading wider and wider, like the Cheshire cat.

"Oh, MK." He shook his head as he rubbed his thumb across his grinning lips. "I've got a thing for virgins."

He looked at me with interest. He specifically looked at my chest with interest, like he was debating the best way to get me out of my sundress.

I crossed my arms over my chest. "I'm waiting until marriage."

He cocked his head, curious but undaunted. "For religious reasons?"

I was shocked that we were still having this conversation. Most guys would have run for the hills by this time. "Are you trying to figure out the rules of some game?"

He leaned back in his chair, smile still in place. "You're the one who keeps putting your cherry on a platter. I was simply enjoying your company."

"You're leering at my breasts," I said.

He shrugged, completely unapologetic. "I've got a thing for breasts. And your body is smoking hot. It's not illegal to look."

He was joking. He had to be joking. I was twenty pounds overweight, thirty if you asked my mother. Christopher was a golden god. He could go after the sure things, like Pancake and Soda Bottle who were waving goodbye as they left the shop. So why was he staying with me?

His eyes were fastened on mine. Intelligence pushing aside the mischief once more. "How are you going to write sex scenes with no sexual experience?"

The moan of a woman from the other room punctuated his question. I bit the inside of my cheek.

I looked up at Christopher, who continued to rub his thumb against his lip as he considered me. The motion was hypnotic. My tongue snuck out and licked at my lips. "Are you going to offer me some experience?"

His eyes zeroed in on my tongue. He pinched the spot on his lip that mirrored where my tongue had just landed on my bottom lip. I shut my eyes as I realized he was right. I had just offered up my cherry on a platter to him again.

"I'm sorry," I said. "I don't know why I said that?"

"I'm not after your panties, MK. You're not my type."

My head jerked back giving me whiplash.

"Physically, yes. But mentally, no. You're a Mrs. Forever. I'm a Mr. Right Now."

"Meaning," I said, "you're not the settling down and marrying kind? Or if you did, you would cheat on your wife."

"I've never cheated anyone in my life." Christopher frowned, looking like a petulant child and reminding me of my sister's boys. "I'll fuck those two girls tonight. They'll both know I fucked the other one. Hell, I'll probably fuck them both at the same time. Might fuck another girl after that. I don't lie to girls to get what I want. I tell them the truth, and if it's not something they want, I move along. I've never forced anyone to do anything... unless they asked me to."

Again, I saw the flash of the devil hidden behind that angelic face.

"Plus," he continued with that Cheshire grin, "I have a short attention span. I couldn't keep all the lies straight in my head."

Why was I still sitting and listening to this guy? And why was I still hearing his voice reining me in from up high on Cloud Nine? He was everything I didn't want in a life partner. Mainly, because he had no intentions of being anyone's life partner. He worked in a sex shop. He drove a fast car and broke the speed limit. He admitted that he slept with multiple women at the same time.

"Most would say I'm more honest than they'd care to hear," Christopher said. "I have no intentions of getting married. That's a condition of having sex with you, right?"

I couldn't respond. My ears were still replaying him talking about having sex with me.

"Therefore, I have no intentions of taking your virginity because that's not a responsibility I'm willing to commit to."

He was right. That was more honesty than I cared to hear. "So, why are you still here?"

"I never met a romance writer before," he grinned, letting go of his serious side. "I'm interested. My mother calls me insatiably curious. So tell me, how do you keep your readers interested with no sex?"

He'd picked up the conversation about my work again, as though we hadn't been discussing both of our vastly different sex lives. My head was spinning from all the directions my attention was being pulled toward.

There was the crescendoing sounds coming from behind the wall. There was the sound of the bell dinging letting customers in. The sound of Holly's cheery voice as she greeted them. And then there was Christopher, sitting before me with an attentiveness I hadn't had since my grandparents passed away a few years ago.

"Relationships aren't all about sex," I said.

He frowned in disbelief.

"They're not," I insisted. "They're about connection and emotion over time. Love happens emotionally, spiritually, before the physical. Victorian and Regency romances were hundreds of pages long with only a kiss on the last page. Yet, it was clear the hero and heroine were in love by the middle. You really know it's true before all the sex clouds your brain."

Christopher grinned. "How would you know that sex clouds the brain?"

"Doesn't it?"

He didn't answer, but I got the distinct impression, even with the mischief in his grin, that his brain never got clouded.

"People get stupid," I said. "Two women are willing to sleep with you, one after the other, or at the same time."

"And you think that makes them stupid? Chrissy is an engineer and Fiona created her own startup. They're two intelligent women who have a sex positive view of their bodies. Satisfaction is a powerful emotion, a relaxing emotion that provides clarity -at least for me."

The crescendoes in the other room were coming fewer and further between, like the last few seconds of a bag of popcorn turning in the microwave.

"If you believe so strongly in what you're doing with the sweet romance," he said, "why change it?"

"Sex sells. And if I want to keep my publishing contract, I have to write about it."

He leaned forward. "But you don't want to?"

I shook my head.

"That sounds like an abuse of power to me."

I couldn't disagree. It was akin to a boyfriend demanding his girlfriend have sex with him or he'd break up with her. I didn't want to break up with my career. I loved what I did. I loved weaving stories of romance, of having two people from opposite spectrums come together, and making their lives together work.

"One thing I do know is that the experience of an orgasm is something you can't plagiarize," he said. "Guys might not be able to tell when a woman is faking it, but another woman can."

He was right about that. I'd watched enough opening scenes of porn to be the judge.

"If you need a hand with writing those parts," he

leaned further forward, bracing his elbows on the table, "let me know. I'll help you."

I pulled back slighty. My hand rose off the table like I was in grade school. "I have to ask again, but I mean it this time. Are you trying to get into my panties?"

He laughed out loud. "I don't have to get into your panties to show you what an orgasm feels like. Give me your hand."

FIVE

My fingers twitched like a nerve had been pinched and was trying to break free. My pinky finger stuck out straight as though struck by lightning. My thumb curled into my palm. The three fingers in the middle flexed forward as though reaching out for Christopher, who watched my twitchy fingers with amusement.

I balled all my fingers into a fist. "What are you going to do?"

His blue eyes locked onto mine and held. If carnal was a color, it would be found in Christopher's eyes. He grinned, reminding me of a puppy dog. "Trust me."

His hand lay open on the table across from mine. Not moving close. Not retreating away.

One by one my fingers unfurled. I watched them in puzzlement, trying to work out why. The scary thing was that I did; I trusted him. There was something about Christopher that told me I could.

Was it those clear blue eyes that hid nothing and let me see his every intention? Was it that mischievous grin that urged me to come out and play? Was it the fact that I had his undivided attention and had somehow managed to hold his interest?

My grandfather always told me that people tell you who they are when you first meet them. The problem was that listeners often choose to ignore the truth. Christopher told me exactly who he was. He'd said it to my face. The question was would I listen?

I placed my hand in his. His was warm. A slight hum of energy zinged between us. He ran his thumb along the sides of my thumb and then my pinky finger. The tremors stopped. A sense of calm flooded through me.

He placed his other hand below mine and continued to graze my skin lightly. "What do you feel?"

Like I was lying in a cradle of warmth. "Safe."

My fingers flexed. I had not meant to say that. But it was what I felt. I'd never had anyone hold my hand as an adult.

I wrote about men holding women's hands. I'd never experienced it in real life. The words I'd written didn't do this simple gesture justice. I couldn't tell him that. So, I did what any writer worth her ink would do. I reached into my writer's toolbox for a metaphor.

"I mean," I tried again, "your fingers are cradling mine. So, it reminded me of the hammock in my grandparents' backyard. I'd lie there for hours reading and no one bothered me. My grandma would bring me honey tea and cheese sandwiches. My grandpa would kiss my forehead as he worked in his vegetable garden. Your fingers are warm and they reminded me of the feeling of the sun on my skin. The hammock was under a tree so when I swung I'd go in and out of the light. With your touch, the pads of your fingers are the warmth, and in between are the clouds. I felt safe in that hammock."

I stopped, realizing I'd dug myself into an even deeper hole with my purple prose. I looked up into Christopher's clear, blue eyes. I couldn't read his expression.

He looked... enraptured? That couldn't be right. It was more flowery nonsense spewing from my writer's tool kit. He probably thought I was some little girl lost.

"Not that I was unsafe anywhere else." I didn't want him to get the impression I came from an abusive family. Dysfunctional, sure. Abusive, no.

Christopher squeezed my palm. He grazed his fingers over my wrist. The sensation shot up my arm like an electric shock, right into my chest. A shudder went down my spine and I let out a trembling sound.

His eyes widened in surprise. Or was that male gloating? He'd gotten me to spew nonsense and now he'd gotten a physical reaction from me. He probably saw a clear pathway to my panties.

I tried to yank my hand away, but his long fingers closed around my wrist. They were light enough to let me know that I could get away. They were firm enough to let me know he wanted me to stay.

"Wait," he said softly. "Tell me what you felt just then?"

His eyes were earnest as they looked into mine. There was no gloating. Only curiosity. Could that be right?

"I like the way you describe things, MK." He grazed the pulse point over my wrist. "It never occurred to me that such a light touch could be so sexy. Tell me? How would you describe that in a book?"

My head spun as my pulse raced. Here was a guy asking me for my favorite thing. He wanted me to tell him a story. There was no way I could resist. I stopped struggling and let him have my hand.

I closed my eyes and pictured the hero in my book. Unsurprisingly, the hero had blond hair and blue eyes. "When his fingers slid down her wrists, her blood wanted to reverse course and follow. His touch stopped my heart and changed the course of my life."

The room fell silent. The chorus of meditative orgasms stopped. No new customers dinged into the door. Holly's cheery chatter muted as well.

I opened my eyes. There was a small smile of satisfaction on Christopher's face. "I meant to say *her* eyes, not *my* eyes."

He tilted his head in acknowledgment, but I didn't think he believed me.

"I stand corrected," he said. "That totally turned me on. And you're not even naked. You're very good."

A tremor went up my palm which still lay in his hand. His hold tightened slightly, just a firm caress. Everything in me slowed. The tremors, my pulse, my heartbeat, my sense of self-preservation. My doubts of who he'd told me he was.

I thrilled at his praise, feeling for the first time that I could do this. I could throw the door wide open and write this steamy book.

"What are you going to do about penetration?" he asked.

And just like that, everything came crashing down.

"Please don't do the crashing waves or any water references," he said. "I don't know any guy who would want his moves compared to a woman drowning."

"I don't know? I haven't gotten that far."

He grinned at the double meaning of my words. I hadn't gotten that far in my intimate life nor in the book's plot.

"You don't need to be penetrated to have an orgasm." His words were thoughtful. He gazed off into the distance, still holding and caressing my wrist and fingers.

A tingling sensation made its way up my arm. My breathing shallowed. I should probably take my hand back. Instead, I pressed my thighs together.

"You could just describe the sensations you feel from masturbating."

He didn't look at me as he said it. But in the silence that ensued he turned those blue lasers back on me. It took him only a second to review the x-ray of my red face and make a diagnosis. I knew it was clearly written on my face that I'd never touched myself in that way.

"I can help you with that," he prescribed. "If you'd like."

"You want to help me masturbate?" I pulled my hand away then.

There it was. He'd been trying to get inside my panties the whole time. I should've known better. I should've listened. I was nothing but a conquest to a guy like this.

"You don't have to get naked," he said, eyes smiling like he'd seen my every thought. "And I won't touch anything you don't want me to. I can get you close to coming just touching erogenous zones that don't touch where your bathing suit does."

I heard this man loud and clear. I believed him. He looked at me with those fathomless eyes, hiding nothing. My fingers, which had balled into another fist, unfurled once more.

But there was no way I was doing this. I couldn't possibly do this. Was I actually considering doing this?

The sound of a whistle cracked the air, muting the ringing of the bell over the shop's open door. A dark figure stood in the door. The same man who had raced down the street with Christopher walked in.

Without his sunglasses on, his hazel eyes did a slow scan of my body, taking his time at the slow curve of my ample bosom on down to my wide hips which took up the whole plastic seat of the chair. He sucked in his bottom lip as his journey reached my thick thighs, which were pressed together under the table.

I wanted to say something, but I couldn't. I thought of any number of sassy quips, but my throat went dry as his eyes heated my limbs. Those blazing eyes stayed on me as he spoke to Christopher.

"Yo, Crow? You ready?"

Crow seemed an odd nickname for Christopher? Why not Chris? Or the more popular Topher?

"No, I'll catch you later," Christopher said, leaning back in his chair. His eyes were also on my breasts. "I'm still working here."

The other man's lip curled into a smile that would make the devil shiver. "She coming to the party tonight?"

Christopher's eyes found mine. The edges crinkled as he gave me all of his focus. "No, she's not like that."

There was disappointment in his voice. There was also certainty. It shouldn't have mattered. I didn't want to go to this party where he was planning to have sex with two or three women.

But part of him wanted me there. That thought thrilled me.

"She looks sweet," said his friend who still hung in the doorway.

"I'll catch you later, Eagle." Christopher tossed over his shoulder.

Eagle turn to head out of the door. "Selfish son-of-a-bitch," he murmured. The ringing bell punctuated his exit.

"Friend of yours?" I asked.

Christopher shrugged. "Just one of my brothers."

I didn't remark that they were of different races.

"How many brothers do you have?" As the words left my lips, I realized that I didn't know this guy. But a moment ago I had been seriously considering letting him touch me where my bathing suit touched me. A moment after that, I'd been contemplating an invitation to a party where he'd be having sex with other girls.

This had been a fun stop in dreamland, but it was time to get back to the real world where heroes sought out their fated mates, fell in love at first sight, and made grand overtures in their apologies for a big misunderstanding.

I gathered my things. "I should go."

"But we weren't finished."

I stopped and looked at him. He was pouting again, complete with the puppy dog eyes. But I saw it. There was the devilish curl to his lip that told me he wanted to make mischief.

"Why didn't you invite me to your party?" I asked.

It wasn't what I had planned to say, but those were the words that wanted to come out. That often happened when I was writing. I'd plot the story, but sometimes the characters hijacked it and took me where they needed to go instead of where I thought was best.

Christopher tilted his head back and peered up at me. "You mean, the party where I'm going to fuck those two girls? It's not your scene, MK. You're not the type of girl to be fucked with. You're a princess looking for a fairytale. I'm not a prince. Neither is Eagle or any of my brothers."

Again, was that disappointment I heard in his voice? Or was it my imagination?

Normally, at this point in my books the hero tells the heroine all the reasons they can't be together.

But over the course of the story, they both grow and change. Is that what was happening now? Was Christopher listing all the ways that he would change? As the pages turned, would we find our way to a happily-ever-after?

"But I do want to give you an orgasm," he said.

I heard the pages crumbling in my head and falling onto the floor with a loud thunk.

"I want to hear what you have to say about it. I like listening to you describe things."

His eyes sparkled, an angel asking for my soul, and I swear to God, that was the moment I lost my heart to the man I knew I would spend the rest of my life with.

SIX

We waited for the last of the Orgasmic Meditation group to file out of the room. Everyone looked peaceful and sedate as they waved to Holly. The golden bell jingled merrily as they left the store.

My grandmother once told me that every time a bell rang, it meant an angel got its wings. Maybe there was an angel presiding over orgasms. If so, was a bell about to toll for me?

I didn't write about orgasms in my books. My characters never got that far. I wrote about soul-piercing gazes, light touches that arrowed to the heart, and kisses that spoke of forever. And I hadn't experienced a single one of those either.

I had had men's eyes on me. I had an ample bosom, so of course they looked. I had men paw at me, wanted and unwanted. I'd had my fair share of kisses, too. But none had ever pierced an arrow aimed at forever like the light hold of Christopher's hand holding mine.

I walked into the room behind Christopher. He shut the door but didn't lock it.

"You can say no or stop at any time, and I will," he said.

His voice startled me. My fogged brain reached to understand his words. His blue eyes held mine. There was no mischief. His gaze was clear, sober, assessing.

"The boss doesn't tolerate anything resembling non-consent. Plus, I would never do anything you don't wish. Are we clear? Do I have your trust, MK? Do I have your consent?"

I nodded hypnotized by his words. He walked over to the far wall and pulled down the blinds. I watched his hands twist the long, plastic stick that turned the blinds to closed, shutting out the bright sunlight of the heavens and casting us down into a muted orange darkness.

"And I have your word that you'll tell me to stop if you're uncomfortable?" He paced towards me. Slowly, like a predator stalking its prey. "Let me hear you say it, MK."

"You have my word," I parroted.

"Then you have *my* trust and *my* consent." Christopher placed his hands in my hair, making firm circles and then combing his fingers through. "Just relax, princess."

His fingers grazed the C-shaped tips of my ears, then pressed over the lobes. I moaned. The sound reverberated from his finger pads back to my eardrums. I heard my heart beating at the base of my ear where his thumb touched.

"I know you don't like water references," I said. "But all I can think about is the sound of the ocean waves washing over me about to knock me down because your touch is so gentle but so powerful at the same time."

He grinned, staring at my lips. I leaned forward, certain this kiss would shout the word forever. But he didn't touch my lips. He skipped my lips.

He massaged my neck. I'd never realized how papery-thin the skin covering the neck was. Everything was magnified. I felt the calluses of his middle finger as it traced the baby hairs at the nape of my neck. In my mind, I saw him holding our newborn baby in his strong, work-worn hands.

His gaze was open, intense as he watched my reaction. "Tell me."

I choked. I couldn't tell him I saw forever in his eyes. I couldn't tell him I'd just had his imaginary baby. That he was cradling the dream child in his arms. That was crazy talk.

It was crazy talk that I wrote in my books that were on Amazon's top selling lists.

"I feel small and vulnerable," I said. "You're bigger than me, and stronger. You could crush me with your hands." He could crush me with a harsh laugh at my altered version of the truth. "But your eyes tell me to trust you. Your gentle touch is soothing. I feel... cradled."

Just like our newborn baby would feel as she looked up at her father for the first time. He would smile at her just like he smiled at me now.

Christopher's hands went down to my shoulders, massaging the caps. My head lolled back as his fingers rhythmically dug into my flesh. I realized that in this position, he had me completely under his control. He could pick me up. He could set me down. He could lead me in any direction he chose. And I wouldn't hesitate to follow.

Instead of moving me bodily, he moved his hands along my body; steadily south. My eyes flared as I pinpointed his destination.

"Is this okay?" His fingertips grazed the topmost

place where a woman's chest became breasts. "You can tell me no, MK."

No. Actually, I couldn't. My body told my brain to shut its mouth. Every cell in my body screamed that this was him; the One.

In the recesses of my brain, something nagged at me, like the buzzing of a tiny gnat. I mentally squashed it and arched into Christopher's patient, skilled, masterful hands. He took his time arriving at his destination. Slipping and sliding down the peaks of my breasts. Circling and tapping at the underside where underwire met flesh.

Other men had felt me up before. I'd never enjoyed the experience. They'd all been a series of awkward squeezes and painful pinches.

Not Christopher.

He lifted my right boob and massaged the skin at the crease. I let out a helpless sound and grabbed onto his shoulders.

"I've got you," he whispered. "Tell me what you feel?"

Like I wanted to cry. "I feel like I'm falling, because of the circles you're making with your thumbs." My voice did not sound like my own. It sounded far away. My words came out choppy. Staccato, like I was speaking over a static radio.

"I won't let you fall, Mary Katherine."

I opened my eyes and slammed right into his blue depths. He was wrong. I fell. Right into him.

Christopher allowed me to lay my head against his heart. My heartbeat synched to his as both his palms covered as much of the surface of my breasts as they could manage. They felt like they were swelling in his hands.

When the fleshy part of his hands, the part at the bottom of his thumbs, met with my nipples, I had to press my thighs together.

"Tell me."

I couldn't tell him what I was feeling in that moment. It was too embarrassing.

"Tell me, princess. Please?"

I couldn't resist him. Not with the way he whispered *please* to me. I would've given him anything in that moment. And so I told him. "I feel like I have to pee."

He reared back, away from me. I was left mortified. I let go of his shoulders and tried to push away.

"Please don't." His voice was so soft, so full of wonder.

My brain had to be malfunctioning. That couldn't be right. I'd just told this guy that when he'd touched my breasts, it made me feel like I had to pee. That had to be disgust in his tone, revulsion.

Instead, I saw awe and excitement sparkling in his eyes. He pulled my torso back to his.

"Please?" he asked again. "Tell me."

I couldn't form words. I couldn't look away from the... was that hope in his eyes? What could he possibly be hoping for?

When I didn't offer any resistance, he took it as acquiescence. He cupped both of my breasts in his hands. Using his thumbs, he began a windshield wiper motion.

The sensation of fullness in my core increased. I pressed my thighs together. When that didn't relieve me, I squirmed, shifting my weight from foot to foot. I had to get out of here before I truly embarrassed myself.

But Christopher held me firm. "Just breathe, princess."

Princess? I latched onto the endearment. He'd said he wasn't a prince. But he kept calling me his princess. With my mind on the fairytale, I let my thighs part and something unexpected happened.

"Tell me." he said like he knew what was happening inside my body but wanted the vocal confirmation.

"I feel..." There wasn't enough air in the room. I took a deep breath, but it made matters worse. My breasts felt like they were spilling out the sides of my fitted bra.

"Tell me, princess." Christopher found both of my nipples through the padding in my bra that seemed threadbare.

"So full," I whimpered. "I'm so full... down there. I have to go." But I didn't make a run for the bathroom. Having to pee never felt this good. It wasn't the fullness that was overwhelming. It didn't feel like liquid trying to make its way out of me. It felt like something else trying to make its way inside me.

"It's spreading," I panted. "It's warm. And heavy. And smooth. I can't stop it."

He flicked both my nipples with his nails and the fullness burst inside of me. Like fireworks, it spread. It wasn't gentle. It burned and singed me from the inside out.

I well and truly fell then. True to his word, Christopher caught me. He brought us down to the pillowed ground. He held me until I caught my breath.

"Was that a...?"

He nodded as he brushed a strand of hair from

my face. His fingers were tender as they placed the strand back where it belonged. I closed my eyes and settled into his care.

Now, I saw what all the fuss was about. I understood why sex made people stupid. I would have failed at school, at my career, probably at life if I'd known something so magical could happen with my body.

"I've never had a woman come from breast fucking," he said as he continued to stroke the side of my face. "That was the hottest thing I've ever seen."

He'd have the privilege of seeing it night after night when we were married and the baby was snug in her cradle.

"Christopher?" Holly's cheery voice called from behind the closed door. "Do you two need a condom? I moved them from the bottom to the top cabinet."

"No, Mom, we're good," he said. "We're just masturbating."

SEVEN

"Mom?" I bolted up. Out of his hold and onto my knees.

"Yeah. Holly's my mother."

The man of my dreams transformed before my eyes. He looked like a little boy then. The curls on his head seemed childish. His blue eyes filled with wide-eyed innocence. I expected his mother to walk in and offer us juice boxes and a snack.

Christopher grinned in a way that was anything but childish. He ran his thick fingers down the side of my face.

"Don't be embarrassed," he said. "She'll be thrilled that we brought you to orgasm."

My face flamed where he touched, and not in

the good way it had a moment ago. I scrambled to my feet.

Christopher lounged back against the pillows. "Do you swear you don't masturbate? Because it's not normal for a woman to come like that, especially a virgin."

I couldn't handle this conversation. I hopped over the pillows and grabbed for the door handle.

"Mary Katherine? What's wrong?"

I yanked the door open. There were a few customers milling around the sex toys and DVD collection. Had they heard me?

Holly looked up and smiled at me. I saw it then. She had the same blue eyes as her son. And they were sparkling at me in the same way. She was thrilled I'd had an orgasm. She'd heard me having an orgasm. Which meant they all had.

I ducked my head, hiding my steaming cheeks. I made a mad dash for the exit. The bell rattled my nerves as I slammed out the door. I didn't stop until I was in my car. Thankfully Lucille turned over on the first try. I took off down the street, going zero to forty in the old jalopy.

My mind reeled. Had it all been some kind of warped sex shop prank? Were mother and son some kind of sick duo that lured girls into the back room to... what? I didn't know. I didn't care.

It had all been too good to be true, right from the start. A handsome guy interested in me like that? Yeah, right, Mary Katherine. These kinds of things only happened in romance novels. Not to girls like me. Chubby virgins who wrote inspirational romance. I was easy prey; low hanging fruit.

They were probably laughing at me. Telling stories to the yoga sex class about the fat girl who got off from her breasts being massaged. Breasts that still tingled from Christopher's touch.

I launched into my apartment and slammed the door behind me. I wanted to cry but my body was too sensitized. I stripped off my clothing; down to my underwear, but my panties were moist.

I got the feeling that Christopher would've laughed at that word; moist. But my brain was too addled to think of another.

I sat on my bed, but I couldn't sit still. I pulled on a robe and sat at my computer. I was a plotter. I spent hours pouring over research. I grafted spreadsheets for plots. I did psychological workups on my heroines, heroes, and villains. But tonight I just started typing.

The story shaped into an ugly duckling trope. A

plain girl and the college jock. It was the typical teen-flick set up. He uses her to win a bet. The joke goes cruelly wrong. She runs off. But in my story he follows her.

As he comforts her, they begin to touch. He takes her hand. Then he touches her ear, then her shoulders, and finally her breasts. She has an orgasm from the breast manipulation.

The words flowed from me as the memories from my time with Christopher flooded my senses. There were no waves crashing. In the story, outside the marching band was practicing. Her orgasms came along the crescendo of the drumbeats.

By the time I finished writing, I was drenched in sweat again. I'd written four solid chapters. I sent it to my editor without doing a spell check.

It was the best I could do. If Moira didn't like it, then maybe Hera would release me from my contract. I had nothing to lose.

The shower's water was a raging flood on my sensitive skin. I could only stand it for a few moments. Orgasms were nothing like water on the body. I totally understood Christopher's point now.

I hit the covers, and I was immediately pulled into a deep sleep.

• • •

I WOKE in the morning with a delicious hum running through my body. My hand rubbed at my chest and my whole body came alive, along with my memories.

I remembered Christopher watching me. Those bright blue eyes that had been so full of mischief... and awe. Those hands that had been so strong... and gentle. That voice that urged me to talk, to tell him a story, to share my feelings.

I tossed my head back down onto the pillows. The feathers let out a puff as my muddled head landed with a thud.

It was late in the morning by the time I rose. I trudged around my apartment. I cleaned the bathroom. I rearranged my closet, putting away the last of the winter items and hanging all of my spring dresses. I reorganized my shoes by heels, wedges, and flats.

I avoided my computer for as long as possible.

It was late afternoon by the time I finally sat down at the screen and prepared to face the world outside. I woke up the screen and waited to connect to Wi-Fi. I watched the inverted triangle go up and down, gaining in signal strength.

There was some fan mail. A few queries from

other authors about joining in on a group promotion. A few bits and bobs of spam.

There was an email from Moira.

I almost avoided it, but my browser was on a setting where I could see the first line of the email. I saw the words *love it* and *want more*. I clicked open.

My eyes grew bigger and bigger as I read. Moira loved the writing I'd done in haste the other night. She thought it was fresh and exactly what she was looking for. Other than a spell and grammar check, the only thing she saw missing was the male POV.

My elation burst and the pieces came crashing down. It was a stretch for me to write that much from the heroine's point of view. To detail someone's first sexual experience outside of a passionate kiss. To detail *my* first sexual experience in such a detailed, unapologetic way.

I hadn't truly thought anyone would want to read it. I hadn't believed it was any good. Christopher had kept asking, no begging, me to tell him more. He'd wanted to hear my carnal thoughts. And now, it seemed, Moira wanted to share them with the world.

Along with the male's point of view on the matter.

I'd never written the male POV before. I had no

clue what men thought. I was a romance writer, not a mind reader. But apparently men's perspectives was all the rage now; dual POV and in the third person.

I'd dug myself into the corner of writing a sexy book. Now, I was deep in the trenches having to convince the reader I knew what men thought. My back was between a rock and a hard place.

And then I saw his email.

At first I thought it was just a new fan. The sender's username was crow@watcherscrew.com. The subject line from the browser read, *I enjoyed meeting you.* That caught my attention because I hadn't done any reader events or conventions in months.

DEAR MK,

I enjoyed meeting you the other day. I picked up one of your books and read it last night. I wasn't too surprised that I enjoyed it. As I'm sure you could tell, I like the way you describe things.

I'm sorry you were embarrassed by what happened between us. I thought it was the most beautiful thing I've ever seen and you should be proud that your body can achieve that kind of reaction.

Most women would kill to be so in tuned with their bodies.

Your breasts were magnificent to hold. I don't know if it was my imagination, but it was like they got bigger the more I touched them. That's probably wishful thinking on my part. I'm dying to know what color your nipples blush. I wonder if they turn the same pink as your neck and cheeks did? My favorite part of our time together was how your breathing changed. I read in your book about hearts fluttering. Your breath did that when you came. I felt the shudders all over your body.

Anyway, I hope we can still be friends. I liked talking to you as much as I liked watching you come. If you need anymore help with your book, hit me up.

~CROW

I felt tingles in my breasts reading his words. My heart pounded in my ears when he reminded me of the flutters I'd felt all over my body. My nipples hardened when I reread the part where he wondered about their color. I wanted him to see that he was right. Even though my hair was brown, my skin was fair and my nipples did turn pink when they hardened. They were likely almost red now.

He wanted to be my friend. My eyes blurred on that word. The letters jumbled and rearranged themselves into something more.

Not only was the man a poet. He'd told the story through a male's perspective. And he'd offered to help me again. It was low hanging fruit. But the question was should I reach for it?

EIGHT

Every girl dreams of her wedding day. In my head, I saw myself standing on a beach.

No, wait. Scratch that. That was my sixteen-year-old dream.

As a twenty-four-year-old woman, I saw myself standing on a hilltop overlooking a body of water; probably a lake. I didn't wear white. Even though I could because, well, I qualified. But it was not the best color on me.

Instead, I wore a light purple, princess-cut gown. The bodice was strong enough to manage my girls. It cinched at the waist and then flowed down my curves giving me a semblance of an hourglass shape. I had a ton of tendrils curling around the nape of my neck. I wore a tiara because my fiancé had a habit of calling me his princess.

But it was a wedding which meant there were some unpleasant parts. My mom would manage the whole thing and be the equivalent of a bridezilla, or whatever the term was for a mother-of-the-bride-zilla. My sister would complain the whole time, insisting that my wedding was costing more than hers. Her children would act out and whine and fidget during the procession. Her husband, if he showed up, would forget to turn off his cellphone. It would ring during the ceremony and he'd disappear to take the business call. My dad would give me away. Later during the reception, he would sneak off with some widow from the groom's side.

But it didn't matter. I understood, even in a dream, that weddings were for the family and friends. Marriage was for the husband and wife. The wedding itself lasted the day, but the marriage, my marriage, would last forever. Just like my grandparents.

I'd never seen Gram and Pop have an argument. They'd never spent the night apart. And they were always there lending support to each other.

In my head my father was already gone from the rented hall. My mother trolled the dance floor complaining about him to anyone who would listen. My sister's husband pulled off in his two-seater convertible to take care of business, leaving my sister to tend to their rowdy bunch all on her own.

But in my dream, standing before my new husband, we'd get lost in each other, not in the chaos. Standing before the reverend, he'd tell us we could seal our vows with a kiss. I would run my hand through my husband's blond hair and-

"Mary Kate, I said we're pushing up your publishing date."

I had tuned out my editor over the phone. With the news she delivered, I tuned her back in.

"We've already been thinking about covers," Moira said. "I hate the whole bare chested, six-pack abs craze. But the hell if it doesn't sell. We'll be booking a cover shoot in the next month."

"Wow, so soon," I said. "I haven't even finished the first draft."

"You've never let us down before," said Moira.

I was out of the slow lane with the new authors and back in the fast lane where I belonged.

"If there's one thing I can say about you, you've never missed a deadline. Not once."

That was true. I was a consummate professional. I'd heard of other authors in the publishing house pushing their due dates back by months. I always had my manuscript in early. I didn't understand what those other authors did all day? My days were spent with my butt in the chair and my fingers on the keyboard.

I didn't have much of a social life. I didn't date often. The men in real life could never compare to the one's in my head. I'd never been one for girls night, much preferring to curl up with a good book and a warm cup of tea.

"Where did all of this inspiration come from?" asked Moira. "Is there a new guy?"

Moira and I weren't the best of friends. We weren't actually friends at all. But I wound up opening my mouth. "It's very new."

Funny that; I said its new, even though in my mind Christopher was completely entwined in my life. I'd had a pretend baby within an hour of meeting him. I had to rewrite that initial story to get the ring on my finger. A week later, in this new fantasy world of marital bliss, we were back from our honeymoon with child number one cooking in the oven.

"The facts always make the best fiction," said Moira. "If you're writing without an outline, I'd like to see the next three chapters soon. And I'm looking forward to reading the hero's perspective."

Right. That.

I got off the phone with Moira and stared at the blinking cursor. My butt was in the chair. My fingers hovered over the keyboard. But nothing came.

I didn't know how to think like a man. In my books, men did everything I told them to do. They first acted aloof, not saying anything to my heroines. They sometimes behaved like jerks. But, I, as their creator always knew they were hiding feelings and leaving their true desires unsaid, just like Fitzwilliam Darcy, the ultimate hero. At the end of the stories, also like Mr. Darcy, the men came up with poetic grand gestures that would wipe my heroines' minds of all the bad times and send her into their arms for a happily-ever-after.

That was simply how things were done in the world of romance.

But with this manuscript, I was supposed to write from the male's perspective. I had no clue how to do that outside of the grand speech at the end. Who knew what men thought day in and day out?

My fingers hovered over the keyboard for a quarter hour. My butt squirmed in my seat. Finally, I switched from my word processing program to a web browser.

Christopher had left his phone number in the email, but I'd hesitated in calling him. His words were lovely and sincere. A great view into the male perspective. There was something between us, I knew it. I'd written enough about chemistry to know when I saw it in real life.

But he was clearly a player. He'd told me to my face that he slept around. I was a smart girl. I knew our fantasy marriage couldn't exist outside of my head.

Could it?

My cell phone rang. I grimaced when I saw my mother's name on the caller ID.

"Principal Stafford was very disappointed not to meet you, Mary Katherine."

"I don't know why? He was your guest not mine."

"He's very handsome," said my mother. "And single."

"Well, that's good for him. I'm sure there will be many female teachers looking out for that. Or single mothers."

"A girl like you could do much worse."

I nearly hung up.

"He's looking for a new English Literature teacher, and since you're unemployed…"

"I'm not unemployed," I rose from my seat and crossed my arms over my chest, tucking the phone between my cheek and chin. "In fact, I signed a new publishing contract."

The phone went silent, but I could hear her roll her eyes and groan. I felt a lecture coming. So, I preempted it.

"And I'm seeing someone."

That may not have been the right thing to say. But at least I didn't get a career goals lecture. Instead, my mother launched into a thirty minute, one-sided conversation trying to draw out the details of my new relationship.

I wasn't seeing Christopher in the dating sense. But I decided I would see him in the literary sense. I pulled up the email with his phone number.

I didn't think my parents would approve of Christopher. His mom owned a sex shop for God's sake. He drove a fast, sports car and not a sensible town car. I had no idea what he actually did for a living -that is, if he worked outside of his mom's shop. Maybe he was unemployed?

Could I be one of those modern women who supported her man? It had ripped apart my parents' marriage. But then again, I saw no joy in my sister's marriage where she was the one supported by her husband who offered her no support in her work as a homemaker.

My mother and sister weren't bad people. Not really. My mother did charity work. My sister was on the PTA and volunteered at a food kitchen for the homeless. Maybe it was my dad and brother-in-law who were the bad guys?

Christopher seemed so self-assured. In fact, he was so self-assured that he thought nothing of getting two women into his bed. Which meant he was predisposed to cheat. I clicked the red X on the web browser, closing his email.

God, what was I thinking?

I knew nothing about this man I'd married and had one and a half kids with in my head. Yes, I was already pregnant with the second. Imaginary-me really liked sex.

In my mind, I packed a bag and backed out of the picket fence. I pushed aside my silly dreams and fantasies of a blue-eyed man with an angelic face and a mischievous grin. In the real world I opened my word processor and went back to my manuscript.

An hour later I was even more frustrated. The

words were not coming. Especially not the words in the male point of view. I still had no clue what men thought. That's why there were always big misunderstandings in my stories. The heroine would misinterpret the hero's intentions until the last chapter of the book where they would finally sit down and have a heart-to-heart where he cleared everything up.

The male character in this manuscript was not following any of the plot points I'd set out for him. I wanted him to chase after my heroine, but he stood in the crowd of his friends watching her with an unreadable expression on his face.

I wanted him to call her up on the phone. But her phone never rang. When I tried to peer into his head, I got nothing.

I had to get this story done. My livelihood depended upon it. I shoved aside my keyboard. I picked up my phone and dialed. It rang four times before anyone answered.

"Watchers Crew Auto and Detailing."

I pulled the phone away from my face and compared the number on the computer screen to the number on my cellphone's screen. I'd assumed this was Christopher's cell phone. But it appeared to be a business line to a mechanic's shop. Was that what he did for a living? It would make sense with the fancy car he drove.

"Is Christopher there?"

"Christopher? There's nobody here named – oh wait. Crow! Phone."

There was audible juggling of the phone, and then I heard his voice clear across the other end of the line. It reached down into the core of my being and lit a fire. It curled up into the top of my head and shined a light on the fantasies I'd tried to turn off.

"MK?"

"How did you know it was me?"

"Only my mother calls me Christopher, and she has my cell number. What's up?"

I took a deep breath and prepared to deliver the speech I'd practiced in my mind.

"Oh wait," he said. "I forgot to tell you."

Forgot? We hadn't spoken in days. But here he was talking to me now like we were old friends that just got off the phone earlier this morning.

"I was watching this movie last night. It was called *A Walk to Remember*. It's based on a book by another author. I don't know his name?"

It was one of my favorite books. I knew the author's name.

"Yeah," Christopher said, "Nicholas Sparks, that's it. It made me think about you."

Christopher was thinking about me when I wasn't there? And he thought about me in the same stream of consciousness with one of my favorite movies and books. In Sparks's book there was a misunderstood bad guy with a heart of gold who befriended and then fell for a shy and modest minister's daughter. The hero gets the minister's daughter out of her shell and helps her find her voice. In return, she becomes his path to redemption.

I wondered what sparked Christopher's comparison between me and Mandy Moore's character? Was it that she was introverted but full of hope? Was it that she turned the hero's bad boy ways around? Was it that she tried new things with him? Things she never imagined herself doing?

"The hot, shy chick was like that character in your book I read. It just sucks that the shy chick dies in the movie. So what's up? How's the writing going?"

"I... it's... I'm blocked."

"You want some help?"

I pressed my thighs together. Beneath my t-shirt, my nipples hardened into tight pebbles.

"I can be over in a couple of hours," he said. "Give me your address?"

I pressed my lips together, but somehow the coordinates to my apartment found a way out. Belatedly, I wondered how he planned to unblock me? Was he coming over to unblock the plot or the barrier to my core? I decided to deal with it when he got here.

NINE

I changed clothes three times, making a wasteland of my closet. I reined my model behavior in when I began contemplating underwear. There was no way this guy would see my underwear. Still, I wore a black lace set beneath a blue sundress that was near the color of Christopher's eyes.

Dressed, I went into the kitchen and marinated two chicken breasts. I chopped some red potatoes and veggies to roast. I chilled a bottle of wine. Then I sat and worried that Christopher would be the kind of guy who drank beer.

I checked the clock. Did I have time to go out and pick up some beer? Did I know what brand of beer a guy like Christopher would drink?

The doorbell rang.

I raced down the hall in my wedge sandals and flung the door open. Christopher stood on the other side. He was dressed casually in jeans and a crisp, white-collar shirt. There was a devilish glint in his eyes and a curl to his lips.

"Hey, MK." He reached out and brought me into his arms. "I missed you," he said into my ear as he squeezed me to him.

Every plan I had went out the door as he stepped into my apartment and closed it behind him. I was thankful I'd worn the nice underwear.

He released me and rubbed his hands together like he was preparing to dig into a hearty meal. "So, where is it?"

"Where's what?"

"The manuscript," he said. "I can't wait to see what you wrote."

"You want to read my first draft?"

"How else would I get you unblocked?"

I broke eye contact, disappointed that he'd come over to help with my work instead of trying to get me worked up.

Through my disappointment, I noticed he had a package in his hand. The package had the logo of his mother's shop on the front. He set it down on the table. "You left this behind the other day."

It was the book and the DVD from the sex shop. I hadn't pulled up another porn website since the day I'd gone to Holly's shop. I couldn't bear to watch those women with the vacant eyes act as though they enjoyed the pounding of those men into their most sensitive areas. Especially not now that I knew exactly how sensitive those areas were. I didn't understand how someone could fake the wonder that was an orgasm.

Christopher walked over to my desk, which housed my laptop. "Is this it?"

He hit a key to wake up the system. It opened to my manuscript. He pulled out my chair, sat down, and started reading.

My feet were immobile. I'd never seen a man read my work. I'd never thought of men reading my work. No one had ever read from my laptop. No one had ever even touched my laptop.

I watched Christopher's fingertips as they caressed the scroll pad. He used his thumb to adjust the angle of the screen for his viewing pleasure. At one point his eyes widened. At another he grinned. Then he laughed.

He turned to me with a grin, then his nose wrinkled. "Is something burning?"

My eyebrows squished together at his question.

My nose wrinkled when I smelled the smoke. I dashed off to the kitchen to save the potatoes. As I set them in a serving dish, Christopher came in.

"It's really good," he said.

I turned with serving spoon in hand. "You finished?"

He nodded. "I learned to speed read when I was a kid. I always wanted to go outside and play sooner. I was home-schooled."

He popped a hot potato in his mouth.

"These are good," he said as he tried to talk and blow and chew at the same time. "You write. You cook. You have amazing orgasms. Is there nothing you can't do?"

The spoon clattered to the linoleum and heat rose up my neck.

Christopher bent down and picked up the spoon. He looked at me with a grimace on his face. "Did I go too far? Sometimes I have trouble with boundaries. If you knew my family you'd understand."

I thought back to his mother who'd smiled proudly at me after her son gave me an orgasm. She'd been congratulating other men and women on their orgasms as they left the meditation class. Yeah,

I could see how boundaries might be a problem in his household.

"Well yes," I said. "It was too far; talking about a woman's orgasms. But I do want to talk with you about it." I swallowed and concentrated on the floor. "Orgasms, I mean. I know what they feel like for a woman -thanks to you. But I don't know how to describe them from the male point of view."

"You want me to describe my orgasm to you?" His lips curled up, and he waggled his eyebrows.

My toes curled and something waggled in my core.

This was not the plan. The plan was to approach this in a businesslike manner. I was supposed to propose that he be my consultant for the research on my manuscript. That was the plan. What came out of my mouth next, I could only blame on the lacy underwear that was a size too small and biting into my skin and cutting off circulation.

"I'll pay you," I said.

Christopher's face fell. The ever-present devil in his eyes was replaced by a wounded cherub. "I'm not a prostitute."

"I didn't mean it like that. I'd be taking up your time; time you could be spending elsewhere... with others."

"I don't mind spending time with you," he said. "I like you. What you do fascinates me. You fascinate me."

It was definitely the circulation-cutting, lacy underwear muddling my brain. My breasts felt like they were swelling in the too small underwire.

"So what happens next in the story?" he asked.

TEN

Christopher had two servings. He also had decent table manners. I'm not sure why that surprised me. Maybe because I kept expecting him to show his true colors and lunge across the table at me, rip my clothes off, and have his way with me.

He didn't do any of that. All of his concentration was on the food before him. He took a mouthful of the chicken. Then used his utensils to slice a potato. Once the spud was in two, he abandoned it to try one of the roasted vegetables. Then he came back to the potato, paired it with a slice of meat, topped it with a vegetable, and took it all in in one bite.

My food sat untouched. Instead, I watched Christopher eat. I watched his tongue test the drippings of my roast. I watched his eyes close as he chewed. I listened to his groans of satisfaction as he swallowed. He licked his fingers after his second helping of everything. With his plate cleaned and his fingers sucked dry, he turned his attention to me.

Particularly, my breasts.

Instead of crossing my arms over my chest, my back arched and my nipples hardened in memory of the last time I had all of his attention on that area of my body.

"So, you're Catholic?" His eyes dipped to my rosary. The cross rested in the valley between my breasts. "That's why you're waiting?"

"No. I mean, yes." My hand went to the cross that rested on my heart. "My family is Catholic, but we're not very good Catholics. The rosary was my grandmother's."

"A rosary," he rolled the words around his tongue. "It reminds me of my auntie's mala beads. Buddhists use them to help focus during meditation. She gave me some when I was a kid, to help me sit still."

"Did they work?"

He grinned, but didn't answer.

"That's not why I'm waiting for... you know." *God, Mary Katherine. If you can't say it, how can you expect to have a conversation about it.* "I'm waiting to have sex after marriage because I want a lifelong commitment with a man. In sickness, health, rich, poor, better or worse. I'm the type of woman who goes all in."

He nodded sagely. "You're looking for your soul mate."

"Yes." I held in a breath and then let it go in a whoosh. "You believe in soul mates?"

"I should. I was raised by two of them. My parents knew they would spend the rest of their lives together when they were kids. They've been together for over forty years now. I know that type of love exists. It's just rare."

My fingers traced the beads of the rosary as I focused my entire being on him. "You don't think you'll find it?"

"I'm not out looking for it. I told you, I have a short attention-span." His eyes held on my chest. I watched the movement of his pupils as I fingered the beads. "Tell me what you need help with? You have more sex questions?"

I felt the flush creep up my chest. Looking down at my chest, I saw the blood shade my skin red.

"Don't be embarrassed, MK. It's not like you're talking to a stranger. We're friends."

"This is only the second time I've met you."

He nodded, his grin full of boyish delight. "Weird, isn't it? I feel like I've known you longer. You want to know about male orgasms?"

I nodded. "My editor loved what I wrote already. But she wants me to tell the story from both the heroine and the hero's point of view. Which means I need to understand what an orgasm feels like for a guy."

His grin was slow. "You want me to orgasm and tell you about it?" His hand roamed down his chest towards his belly. "Do you want me to take care of it? Or did you want to try?"

He must've seen my hesitancy because then he said, "Same rules, MK. *No* means no. *Stop* means immediately. Nothing you don't want to happen will happen."

That was the problem. I wanted things to happen. I wanted him to touch me. I wanted to touch him.

Without words, we rose and moved from the dining area to the living room couch. We sat and his hands reached the divide where his shirt was tucked into his pants. He tugged the tail free, pulled a few buttons loose, and then dragged the shirt over his head.

I had to clutch my rosary, otherwise I may have

reached out and grabbed him. Christopher was perfection. He put every single male, romance cover model to shame with the sculpture that was his abs.

"You wanna feel?" he asked. "You know, to describe it better."

My palms sweat. I reached my hands out to him. His skin trembled at the first whisper of my touch. I looked up, startled. His grin was lazy.

"Your fingers are so fucking soft," he said. "Makes my skin feel thin with your fingers on it. You feel me trembling, princess? It's because I'm excited. You know what else excites me? The sound of a zipper being pulled down. Do you want to do it?"

I looked at his zipper like it was a toothy monster.

"You can say no."

"You keep saying that," I said.

"And I mean it. If you said no I'd be disappointed. I've been thinking about touching you again. I've been dreaming about you touching me. But if you stopped right now, we'd still be cool."

"This doesn't sound like any friendship I've ever had."

His grin turned sultry. "I'm very close with my friends."

A gong went off in my head. I knew he heard it.

The reverb brought to mind the twins from the sex shop. Had they come over that night? Had he had sex with them? Who else had he had sex with in the last week? What the hell was I thinking getting involved with this guy?

Christopher watched me, but he didn't do anything. He didn't say anything to deter my thoughts. He just waited for me to make a decision.

I wanted to be close to this man. I wanted more than his friendship. I presented him with boundary after boundary. He'd simply hold out his hand and ask if I wanted to cross the line. But along with the offer of his hand, he'd warn me that I wasn't the only one who's hand he'd hold.

I had to stop pretending this was anything but what it was. I opened my eyes to reality. I needed this encounter for my research, so I could do my job and keep my livelihood.

"My favorite part is the anticipation," he said. "That's what a zipper sounds like to me; a countdown. I'm throbbing right now and twitching. Do you want to see a visual, MK? You can say no."

"No. I mean... Yes. Can I see?"

He hefted himself out. I'd seen men's penises in artwork, on television, on the Internet. But Christopher's penis was a thing of beauty. It wasn't just a single color. The base of it was a dark shade of pink. The length of it was tan, and the tip was bright pink. For some reason my mind focused on the colors and not the fact that I was staring at a man's penis.

"Do you want to touch it?" *It* jerked towards me. Christopher chuckled as he took it in hand, like pulling on the leash of a dog. "It has a mind of its own. But I'm not the type of man who's led by his dick. I'll only do what you want. I know your boundaries. I won't cross them. I promise."

He didn't need to cross them. I was the one hopping over every line I drew.

He continued to stroke himself as he waited for my answer. His eyes roamed my body as his fingers gripped his length. The tip of his penis seemed to become engorged and turned even pinker.

"It looks like a lollipop," I said.

He groaned and closed his eyes. "Fuck, Mary Katherine, this is the sexiest dirty talk I've ever heard."

I swallowed, my throat filled with an abundance of saliva. I hadn't been trying to talk dirty. I hadn't meant to say anything at all.

"Please, keep going." His fingers played with the tip, playing peek-a-boo with that single eye at the center while the long, thick stick of him continued to jerk.

"No," I said. "You're supposed to be the one talking. I don't know what this feels like."

His eyes, which had become hooded, focused on me. "Will you help me?" He let go of himself and reached out his hand.

Like a puppet I gave him mine.

He shook his head. "Spit in it first."

I frowned.

He grinned, waiting for me to comply.

I did as he told me. He took my hand, like a greedy kid snatching the last piece of candy in the dish. He wrapped my fingers around his shaft. He held my hand there with his strong grip.

"What does it feel like?" he asked.

"Warm, throbbing. It's softer than I expected."

"Your touch is too light. It's driving me crazy. Hold me tighter."

I did as he asked. "I can feel your veins." I ran my index finger along one of the vessels.

Christopher closed his eyes and sighed.

"I feel your pulse," I said. "You *are* trembling."

"Because you're about to make me come."

My mouth went slack and so did my grip. But he

didn't let me pull away. His eyes opened. He stared at me. A question on his brow.

Was I telling him no, the brow asked.

I firmed my grip. His eyes shuttered closed, and he moaned.

"Tell me what it feels like?" I asked.

He grinned. It reminded me of a cat rolling onto its back and offering its belly for a scratch.

"I feel this tingling sensation," he said. "I can't pinpoint where it begins, just somewhere deep inside. It's moving to my balls. It's heavy... like a fullness."

"Like you have to pee?"

"Hmm."

That was exactly what I felt when he made me come.

"It's building, and you know on the other side is relief. You start running towards it." He thrust his hips up into our joined hands. "What's about to happen... is my body is going to start clenching. Like my whole body, not just my dick and my balls. I'm going to thrust mindlessly and then, for like about thirty seconds, everything is going to seem so clear. I'll feel like I could solve world peace. But it only lasts for a minute and then it'll feel like I got hit by a fucking car."

With his free hand, he pulled me to him. He buried his face in the valley of my breasts.

"Can I put one in my mouth?" He nuzzled aside the rosary to get at my breasts.

I arched into him mindlessly. His tongue dove beneath the fabric of the top of my dress and licked at my right breast. Something tightened in my core.

"I want you to come with me, MK."

"Simultaneously?"

He let go of my breast and laughed. "Yeah," he licked at my left breast. "We'll do it together. Hold me tighter and I'll get you off."

I held him tighter. He nudged aside the fabric of my top until all that bordered us was the lace of the bra. It was no real barrier to the magic of his tongue and lips.

We were in a tight clench. I was half on top of him. Our hands between us. There was a bit of action near my pubic bone. If he'd suggested it, would I have let him cross that final boundary? I didn't get a chance to wonder because my body was clenching and so was his.

It was just like he said. The tension built, and this time, instead of trying to get away from it, I ran to it. Head first.

On some level it was like running into a brick

wall. My orgasm was not gentle. It slammed into me. It rocked me from my head to my feet.

I gasped. Then I screamed as my core clenched so hard it caved in on itself. The contractions shook me so thoroughly that I fell backwards.

Christopher caught me. He caught me and he brought me into his arms, against his chest.

He held me to him as we caught our breath. After long moments, he shifted his hips, and we came face to face. He had a cheeky grin.

I leaned into his face, aiming my lips for that grin. He halted me. I saw the surprise on his face. My entire body flushed, but not in the good way.

"Oh my God." I scrambled off him. "I'm such an idiot."

"MK...?"

"That didn't mean anything to you, did it?" I pulled my top up. "I'm just another twin to you, only there's just one of me."

Christopher halted my hands. His grip was not a vice, but it was firm enough to get my attention. "MK, wait-"

"You were just using me. You just wanted to get off."

"Hey, hey." He ducked and bobbed his head until he caught my eyes. "Yes, I wanted to get off.

And I wanted to get you off, too. That's what we both wanted."

I looked away from him. I wanted more than that. I'd tried to mark a clear line in my head, but I'd lost track of the border the moment his tongue struck my nipple. I wanted the fairytale to be real.

"No, MK don't do that. Remember what I told you? I'm not a prince. The things you want, marriage, fidelity, monogamy, I'm not interested in those things."

"You're just interested in my breasts because I can get off like that. You'll kiss them but you won't kiss my lips because..."

"Because what?"

Because I couldn't compare physically to Pancake and Soda Bottle.

I didn't answer. I didn't want him to answer. When he did, his answer was not what I expected.

"Kissing is a boundary for me," he said. "Just like you're not ready for any man to stick his penis in your vagina, I'm not ready for a woman to stick her tongue down my throat. May sound strange, but kissing is a level of intimacy I'm not prepared to offer."

What we did, his penis in my hand, that wasn't intimate?

"This is my fault," he said. "I should've known better. I went too far. I wanted another taste of you and I saw a way to get it. It was selfish and I'm sorry. I hope you can forgive me, but I'll understand if you can't. Or won't."

He stood and turned away from me as he tucked himself back in his pants and pulled his shirt on. When he turned back around all signs of mischief were gone. He looked solemn and sad.

"I want to help you with your work," he said. "But you have to understand, princess, I'm not the guy of your dreams. Don't go falling for me or anything. I'd catch you, because you're my friend. But I'd set you back on your feet, not carry you off into the sunset."

He leaned in and kissed me on my cheek. "I'm sorry I've upset you. I'm going to go now. Call me if you need me, okay?"

He didn't give me a chance to answer. He opened the door and then he was gone.

ELEVEN

"You lost the magic."

My hands sweat as I held the phone to my face and listened to Moira discuss the latest submission of my next few chapters.

"It starts off great. I don't usually like masturbation scenes, but this one was hot."

After Christopher left three nights ago, I wrote like mad. The hot scene she referred to was pretty simple to write. It flowed through my fingers as smoothly as I'd stroked Christopher's hard, thick, veiny cock.

"But after the masturbation scene, everything goes south," Moira said. "In the male POV, this doesn't sound like any guy I know. You have him pledging his love at only a quarter of the way into the book. No real guy would do that."

Not unless they lived in my head. I'd thrown myself at a guy who I'd known less than a week. And like he'd promised, he'd caught me and set me back in my place on the sofa. But in my book, he swept my heroine off her feet and pledged to her his soul.

"It's completely unrealistic, Mary Kate. Plus, there's no tension. She gets everything she wants. The story is basically over as soon as it begins. There needs to be conflict, you know that."

God, I was so sick of conflict. Why couldn't a book just be girl meets boy, they fall in love, and live happily-ever-after? No cheating to prove his manhood. No working late nights leaving her alone to tend the children. No hurdles, or twins, to jump over.

"Plus, this penetration sex scene is so cold," Moira continued. "It reads like insert tab A into slot B. You wrote a beautiful first kiss, a scorching hot masturbation scene. But then what happened?"

What happened was I still had an un-popped cherry. I hadn't called Christopher. I couldn't. I was embarrassed and my feelings hadn't gone away. My body betrayed me every night as I dreamed of him and woke with soaked sheets; my nipples hardened and aching for him. My core clenching and begging to be filled by him.

"Mary Kate, we're counting on you," said Moira. "I have everything locked into place. Was I wrong about you? Is this too much for you? Can you do this?"

"I can," I said. "It's just a rough patch. I know how to fix it."

Moira disconnected and a monotone dial tone filled the line. I terminated the line, sat my phone down, and pulled my laptop towards me. I hit the delete key on large paragraphs of words. But at the end of my search and destroy mission, I still had no clue how to fill the void.

I knew how sex worked, of course. I'd tried watching the Candida Royalle DVD. There was no mugging the camera. But there was still a disconnect, something impersonal about those performances on the screen. Something fake in each person's countenance because they were acting on some level. The story lines were plausible and easy to follow. The scenes were pretty, the lighting beautiful, the editing seamless, the actors attractive. The performances were better than Internet porn, but there was still no connection. These people were fucking, not making love.

It was the same thing that was missing in my books. The parts Moira connected with, I had personal experience with. The parts she rejected, I had no connection to offer. I looked at my phone sitting silent on my desk.

Was I seriously considering giving up my virginity to save my career?

Did I have to?

Christopher said he could show me things without crossing that line. I had no reason to distrust him. He'd been true to his word with everything he'd promised. I was the one who kept crossing the red lines I drew.

The words came alive when I described things to him. He said he would help me, that he wanted to be friends. It was me that had the problem. But I could get it under control. I had to, or my career was over.

I did a quick Google search and found the address I needed. I'd meant for our relationship to be about business the last time we met. My mistake was meeting on home turf. This time I'd meet Christopher at his place of business.

Outside, Lucille started up without incident and we headed across town. I pulled up to the car shop. WATCHERS CREW AND AUTO, the sign read. It sat in the middle of a mixed industrial and residential neighborhood. I parked Lucille in one of the open slots of the storefront and went into the glass front doors.

Inside there was a tall, dark drink of water bent over a car. He had his shirt off. I had trouble averting my gaze from the valley between his abs and his belt buckle. Looking up, I saw grease stains on his muscled chest.

"You're the piece of sweet meat Crow's been pouting about."

There was so much to unpack in that sentence. My hackles went up at being called a piece of meat, regardless that he'd tacked on *sweet* as an adjective. But my attention was diverted to the end of a sentence.

"Christopher was pouting about me?" Every business-minded thought, all pep talk points, all firm red lines, went out of my head.

The guy rolled his eyes. "He's not here. He'll be back soon." His gaze raked over my body. "I'll keep you company until he gets back."

I wasn't afraid of him. I knew he was trying to get a rise out of me. This was one of Christopher's friends. I remembered him from last week at the sex shop.

"Leave her alone, Eagle," said a woman's voice.

Eagle turned to look over his shoulder. "You telling me what to do, sweet meat? I got something for that ass later."

The woman skirted his slap with a giggle and came to stand before me. "Mary Katherine? I'm Eleanor. You can call me Ellie."

Ellie looked like someone from my grandparents' church. She had on a prim and proper blouse and a knee-length skirt. Her blonde hair was pulled into a plaited bun.

"You want to come up to the house and wait?" she asked.

I followed her out the door. Eagle watched us with a narrowed gaze. My instinct was to cover my ass with my hands. Ellie wiggled her hips.

"Crow has never brought a girl home," Ellie said once we were outside on the path that lead from the shop to a three-story house.

"I wasn't invited," I said. "I just need to talk to him about something."

"Is this about your book?"

"He told you about my book?"

I felt irrationally jealous. This girl was basically me. She had good girl written all over her heart-shaped face and prim clothes that were in a slimmer size than mine. But I had nothing to worry about. She was with the shirtless guy, Eagle.

"I'm the only other person in the house who reads anything besides car magazines," Ellie said. "Owl reads literature, but he wouldn't be caught dead reading a romance novel."

Eagle? Crow? Owl? There was an emblem with wings coming out of a tire over the top of the shop. I wondered what was with all the bird names? I also wondered who else lived in this house?

I saw sports cars in the driveway that were straight out of the *Fast and Furious* movie franchise. And there was also a VW Bug with a ladybug paint job. Ellie ran her hand lovingly over the Bug as we headed up the driveway.

"I read your books," she said. "The *Tender Kisses* series is one of my favorites. It's hard to find good inspirational romance that doesn't hammer you over the head with scripture."

"Thank you," I said.

"That's the cutest dress, by the way."

I ran my hands over my sundress. Today it was the color of the sun, a bright and blinding yellow to compliment this beautiful cloudless day. "Thank you."

"I wish I had the curves to carry that off. But as you can see, I'm built like a twelve-year-old girl."

"Are you kidding? I'd kill for your legs. The way my thighs rub together I could light a match."

Ellie let out a bark of laughter. I turned to her expecting mockery. Instead, I saw genuine delight and not an ounce of judgment. She pulled the door open and let me precede her.

Inside, the house resembled a bachelor's pad with a woman's feminine touch. There was dark leather furniture with splashes of color, like couch pillows and coasters.

"Crow and Hawk will be back soon." Ellie led me down the hall and into the kitchen.

"Hawk?" I asked.

"That's my boyfriend."

"But I thought the other guy, Eagle, was your boyfriend?"

Ellie smiled. She opened her mouth. Thought better of it. Then headed for the fridge. "Are you hungry? I was going to make lunch for everyone. Well, not make it myself. I was going to assemble it from leftovers. Crow made a roast turkey the other night. I was going to make sandwiches."

Crow cooked?

"You don't have to go through the trouble," I said.

Ellie shrugged. "Cooking is the love language in this house. Since you're spending time with Crow, you'll probably be around a bit." She smiled at me, seemingly thrilled by the prospect of my continued company.

As she pulled out the makings from the fridge, the door opened to the sounds of masculine voices. A large man entered. He had to turn sideways to fit his bulk into the door. He swooped Ellie into an embrace and a wet kiss.

"MK?"

I turned expecting annoyance. But Christopher looked thrilled to see me.

"I'm so glad you came over," he said. "I missed you." He came over and embraced me. Without the kiss. "Are we good?" He looked so earnest and hopeful.

"We're good." How could I say otherwise?

His grin spread to my heart, and I was right back to where I started.

"So this is your..." Hawk's eyes undressed me as he stroked Ellie's hair. "... friend?"

"Hawk, this is MK," said Christopher. "MK, this is my brother, Hawk. And you already met Ellie."

"And Eagle," Ellie supplied as she leaned into Hawk's chest. "Owl stayed over at Kira's. You guys hungry? We're making lunch."

I didn't remark that none of these men resembled the other in any way. Eagle was African-American. Hawk looked as though he'd sailed from Spain with Columbus. And then there was the golden-haired Christopher.

The men took the utensils out of Ellie's hands and shooed her into a seat as they prepared lunch for us.

With the sandwiches made, Christopher grinned at me over his food. Hawk only had eyes for Ellie. He fed her, then kissed her, then stroked her hair.

"What brought you over, MK?" Christopher asked. "You having trouble again? With the masturbation scene?"

I coughed, nearly choking on a piece of turkey. "Can we talk about this in private?"

"There's no privacy in this house," he said.

Ellie's smile was sympathetic. Then Hawk captured her lips.

I turned away from them. "That scene is fine. It's the... next scene I'm having trouble with."

Christopher nodded sagely. "He's ready to pop

her cherry. Did you read the book and watch the video from my mom's?"

"I did, but..."

"Let me guess, it was all impersonal. I figured that would happen. You write emotion better than action."

He stared off into space pondering my problem.

"Well, you and I can't," he said, motioning between us. "But I have an idea. Hawk, Ellie want to help out?"

TWELVE

I sat in the living room and watched Hawk undress Ellie. She reached for his zipper. Her fingers, practiced and sure, jerked the tab down. The buzzing sound cracked the air. My chest tightened as each tooth of the zipper unclenched.

I turned to Christopher who sat beside me. His nostrils flared at my slow exhale. He looked like he knew what was going through my head.

How could he have any idea what was going through my head? My mind was a fog watching a live sex demonstration.

"Why are you wearing these boxers?" Ellie chided. "I thought I got rid of them."

Hawk swatted away her hand and toed out of his jeans. "You did. They're new."

Ellie turned to me, one eyebrow quirked as though asking me to feel her pain. I couldn't hold her eyes. Her left breast was exposed. The pink bud stared at me before her boyfriend palmed it.

This was nothing like the opening porn scenes I'd seen on the internet where the woman undressed herself while playing with her nipples or looked suggestively at the camera. It wasn't like the Candida movies with the great lighting, smooth camera moves, and intricate plot points. Even though we were clearly in their line of sight, Hawk and Ellie weren't performing. They were completely into each other.

Hawk peeled Ellie's skirt open and then down her long legs. There was nothing adolescent about her body. Hawk sank to his knees. It was an act of reverence. He looked up at her with an expression so powerful I had to glance away.

But only for a moment.

I couldn't stop watching. The love between them was like a thick fog. I swiped at my eyes, and when I pulled my hand away, I watched Hawk plant light kisses on Ellie's midriff. Ellie ran her fingers over his scalp, a soft smile on her face.

Hawk took off Ellie's panties, exposing her intimate flesh. I had trouble changing in front of girls in gym class. I'd never seen another woman's vagina up close. It was probably the look on my face that turned Ellie's smile upside down.

"Is this too much for you, MK?" she asked. "We can stop and talk."

Her expression was full of concern and compassion. She was naked in front of me while her boyfriend's manhood tented with eagerness. No one seemed to think it was out of place.

"Are you guys, like, exhibitionists?" I asked.

"No." Ellie cocked her head to the side. "I don't know? Maybe I am? I don't expose myself out in public. I don't mind an audience. I actually like having an audience. But only of people I know and like."

Her smile at me was inclusive. Then her gaze went thoughtful. Hawk stood and rounded her. He kissed her neck.

Ellie cocked her head to the other side to allow him full access while she kept talking. "Maybe I'm a Candaulist exhibitionist; that's someone who likes to expose themselves in a sexually provocative manner. Or maybe I'm more a Martymachlian-"

"El," said Hawk. "You're going nerdy, babe."

She ignored him. "We're technically swingers

because I only have a love relationship with Hawk. But we have recreational sex with friends."

"Your boyfriend can have sex with any girl he wants to? On the side?" I asked.

"No, that's cheating," Hawk answered with two handfuls of Ellie's breasts. "I don't do anything I wouldn't feel comfortable telling Ellie about before-hand or afterwards."

"I had a hard time with it at first," said Ellie as she leaned into his embrace. "It was confusing. My heart clearly belongs to Hawk." She turned to Christopher. "But I do love the way Crow sucks my nipples."

"Ah, El," grinned Christopher. "You say the sweetest things."

In my lap, my right hand balled into a fist. With my left hand, my fingers found the beads of my grandmother's rosary. "You guys have done that before?" I asked. "Recently?"

"It's just sex," Hawk said. "Sex is fun. Especially with another person. Or a group of people."

I pressed my lips together, but the words escaped nonetheless. "But you love her."

Hawk's gaze turned to Ellie. He grinned like a middle school boy with a love note in his back pocket. It was clear he was head over heels.

I rolled a bead between my thumb and forefinger. "I don't understand how you can watch someone you care about be intimate with another person." I avoided Christopher's gaze, but I knew he was watching me. He kept silent, letting me work this out on my own.

"Because you're still thinking of it like it's cheating," said Ellie, standing naked and unashamed before me. "Polyamory is the norm in the animal kingdom. Monogamy has only come into play within the last millennia. It's widely failed and-"

Hawk captured her lips. "Ellie, I'm going to fuck you now."

He bent down and suckled her breasts. When he did, his ass was to me. I saw the tip of his cock between his legs. I tried not to stare, but I was finding penises hypnotic. Hawk's cock jerked and twitched like a pendulum, a carnal hypnotist putting me in a trance.

Looking up, I saw Hawk flick Ellie's nipple with the tip of his tongue. It was the exact same move Christopher had done to me. Ellie gasped as I had done then. As I did now.

I clutched the beads at my chest. My fingers swiped at the tops of my breasts and I shuddered. I'd felt the sensations she was feeling. Now, I was seeing them up close. My memories and vision collided, and it felt like it was happening to me.

I'd felt nothing looking at the porn videos. Ellie wasn't acting. She smiled down at Hawk, love clear in her eyes. Her head tilted back. She closed her eyes. She didn't swipe her hair out of her face and look around to find the camera lens or moan for the audience.

Beside me, Christopher stretched out, a small smile on his face as he watched Ellie. But his attention was on me.

"Tell us what you see," he said.

The voice that filled the room sounded nothing like my own. But it was mine.

"Her nipples are like pebbles. Her skin is flushed. Her entire chest is turning pink. I can see it spreading in real time, like a shadow of passion."

Hawk looked over at me and smiled appreciatively, appearing to enjoy my descriptions.

Ellie's eyes opened and focused on me.

"This is so interesting," she said. "I've only ever examined sex from a theoretical, quantitative standpoint. Your lyrical, qualitative perspective is fascinating."

Hawk laid Ellie on the coffee table and spread

her thighs. His eyes were on me. "What does it look like?" he asked.

I looked to Christopher. There was pride in his eyes, like it was me and my words that were on display and not Ellie's naked body.

I had to blink a couple of times. All eyes were on me waiting for my words. Hawk lined himself up with Ellie's entrance.

"It looks like a flower stem," I said. "And the flower blossom. The arch of her back is like a valley, her breasts are like mountains."

"That shit's poetic," said Hawk. "Flowers and mountains and valleys."

I hadn't thought of that. Her breasts were like mountains and the curve down towards her core was a valley. "Can I use that in my book?"

"Of course," Hawk grinned. "I like to share." He entered Ellie in one hard thrust.

I couldn't believe we were having a casual conversation as he fucked his girlfriend. Hawk set an unhurried pace. Ellie closed her eyes and put her arms behind her head like she was settling in for a relaxing ride.

I watched Hawk thrust in and then out of her, slowly, deeply. Ellie sighed; her hand went to his bicep. She hitched her leg up. I watched Hawk's angle change and the last inch of his penis disappeared fully inside of her.

"Hey, MK."

I tore my gaze from the union at their hips and up at Hawk.

"Watch," he said. "She's about to come. Watch how her back arches. It's fucking beautiful. Watch how her toes curl. Can you see it? Is that not the sexiest damn thing you've ever seen? A damn pinky toe. Watch her."

Hawk took one hand and moved it southward. His fingers parted Ellie's labials, and he found her swollen clit. He flicked at it and Ellie jackknifed.

I'd seen the women in the videos go through their performance of coming. I'd felt the real sensations myself. But watching another woman having a real orgasm took it to a whole other level.

Ellie's eyes widened, and then closed. Her body jerked, then stilled, then jerked again. I saw the tremors run up her leg. I saw her nipples turn to hard points. She moaned low and then panted as her body convulsed. Her gasps came higher and faster. Hawk fused their lips along with their bodies.

The air around them was charged. It became electrified as Hawk pumped into Ellie. Her cries were desperate. His groans pained. They stared into each other's eyes. Heat from their bodies hit me like a wave. I couldn't look away.

This was love. This was what was missing from the videos. Ellie came again, her face crumbling, her eyes tearing. Hawk watched her, his face contorting in joy. But he didn't stop. He kept going, pumping inside her.

"Please, Hawk," she begged.

He shook his head, no. "I want another one."

He reached down and grabbed her ass, pulling her legs up and over his shoulders. The angle put her completely at his mercy. Her head fell back. Her body went limp and helpless. He pounded into her like a jack hammer.

"You good, MK?" Christopher asked.

I didn't answer.

"You get what you need?"

I turned to him but I still couldn't make any words.

"They'll be at this for a while. We can go to my room... So you can write down some notes."

I should say no.

He knew I should say no.

We both knew that neither one of us wanted me to say no.

Ellie was coming for the third time. Hawk thrust

into her with a guttural yell. Ellie's head rolled back, her mouth in a grin. Hawk's forehead rested beneath her chin in supplication. When Ellie opened her eyes they sparkled.

She grinned at me and waved. "I hope that helped."

THIRTEEN

"Are you okay?" Christopher shut the door to his bedroom. His room was neat and orderly. The bed was made. A navy blue comforter lay folded down at the foot. I walked over to his dresser. There were a few pictures on his dresser top. No one was alone in any of the photos. There was always a group. I recognized his mother in several photos.

"It's still hard for me to understand how they could share that." I touched his face in the glass of one of the picture frames. "It's evident they love each other."

"You share your writing. It's intimate, from your heart. You let hundreds, thousands of people read it. They're your innermost thoughts, fears, and desires. And you let them all in."

Adjectives, verbs, and nouns swam in my brain but I couldn't grasp on to any one for a response.

"Can you use any of that, with Ellie and Hawk, for your book?" he asked.

I nodded, crossing my arms.

Christopher came up and wrapped his arms around me. "You cold?"

"Confused. You say were just friends. But you hold me like I mean something to you."

"You do mean something to me, MK."

"I want more." I squirmed to get out of his arms, but it was a halfhearted attempt.

"Do you want to go home?" His arms tighten around me.

"No." This time I did break away. "That's the problem."

He brought me back into his embrace. I held onto him tightly, like my life depended on it. But I didn't want to be this girl. I didn't want to cling to a man who didn't want me, who wouldn't be there for me.

"I should go." I broke free from him again.

He caught my hand. "Talk to me."

Our fingers entwined. His thumb brushed the center of my palm.

"I have feelings for you beyond friendship," I said.

"I think I have the same feelings. I wanted to call you every day. I missed talking to you. I missed hearing your voice. I want to tell you everything that's been happening with me since the last time I saw you. Is that weird?"

"No," I shook my head. I wanted to do the same thing.

"MK, I want to kiss you."

I couldn't breathe. I had to play his words over again and again to make sure I hadn't made them up in my head.

"But that's not all," he continued. "I want to play with your breasts. I want to put my hands down your panties. And then my face."

My brain reeled and swirled at the impact of his words.

"We don't have to do any of that. We could just hang out," he said. "That's what you do on a date, isn't it? You get dressed up in one of those cute dresses, with your heels on, and your hair out. It drives me crazy when you put your hair up. I want to pull it down."

He reached behind me and pulled my hair-tie

loose. My hair spilled over my shoulders. Just because my hair spilled down my shoulders didn't mean I let go of my senses. I ran all of his words through my head again and picked out the most important one.

"You want to date me?" I asked.

"Yes," he said as he ran his fingers through my hair.

"But you still want to sleep with other women?"

"Yeah," he nodded. "You're not ready for sex and I would never pressure you."

Again I ran the words, like an accountant triple checking their math, trying to make it add up. "So you would go out to dinner with me and come home and have sex with another girl?"

He cocked his head in confusion. "You'd rather I become abstinent?"

"I'd rather you wait for me." My voice sounded like it had when I was twelve-years-old, shrill and crackling its way through puberty.

"You mean marriage?" He let go of the strands of my hair and stepped back. "I said I won't pressure you into sex, but you want to pressure me into a life-long commitment?"

I stepped back, too. There was only two feet between us, but it felt like a gulf.

"I want you in my life, MK. I know that much. I'll give you my time and my attention. I'll respect your desires and beliefs. But I'm not willing to be celibate. I like kinky things that I know you're not ready for, may never be ready for."

He stepped into me, closing the gulf in one step. "When you've dated before, you didn't have sex. So, let's just keep sex off the table."

There had to be something wrong with my hearing. Here was a guy, a very viral guy, who wanted to date me for my witty conversational skills. But the sex we wouldn't be having he'd have with other girls.

"You can say no," he said.

I wanted to stomp my foot. No, I couldn't. I couldn't say no.

I wanted him.

All of him.

"That's everything I have to give you, MK."

Was it enough? He was everything I wanted, minus the desire to play in other women's vaginas. In my books, I spent hundreds of pages with characters talking and getting to know each other before they would kiss at the end. Christopher wanted the intimacy of kissing now, in the middle of our story.

He caught my chin and lifted my gaze. "You can say no, and if you do, I won't bother you again."

"No."

His face fell at the misunderstanding and my heart choked.

"I mean I don't want to say no," I clarified. "I can't seem to say no to you."

"Yes, you can."

He captured my lips. The brush of flesh was so light I could've imagined it. The whisper of his breath was the only real thing I could grasp onto, and it blew by me before I could catch it.

"Do you want me to stop?" he asked, his lips hovering over mine.

"No," I sighed.

"See."

His grin spread across my lips. His tongue tasted the divot at the center of my upper lip. My lips parted on an inhale. Christopher's tongue stole into my mouth. His lips sealed over the breach so that neither of us could escape.

I'd been kissed before. Tentative pecks on the cheek. Stiff tongues swiping my mouth like windshield blades. Sloppy, open-mouthed French kisses. Every last memory of those sophomoric attempts faded from my memory as Christopher owned my mouth.

When he released the bond of our lips, I groped in the darkness. My eyes were open, but the haze of desire blinded me. Christopher moved to my neck and began a slow trail of soft kisses southward.

"You want me to stop?" he asked.

"No," I whimpered.

He shifted the bodice of my dress and kissed the heated tops of my breasts. My nipples were already painfully hard. The flesh beneath and around my breasts swelled until I felt the lace of my bra straining. I swore I heard the fabric tearing.

"Do you want me to stop?" Christopher asked. His mouth hovered over my nipple.

"No."

He reached around my back for the zipper to my dress. "You trust me, princess?"

The sound of the metal teeth unclenching fried my brain. My heart was in my throat and words couldn't get through.

"I know where your boundaries are," Christopher said. "I won't cross them. You *can* say no."

He pulled the dress down my shoulders. His lips led the way. The fabric followed close behind. When the dress came over my stomach, I froze and caught it.

"Is that a no, MK?"

"No -I mean. No one's seen me naked before."

"I feel sorry for every man in the entire world." His hands hovered over my curves. His eyes were big as his gaze took me in. His breath tickled my belly button as he looked at me like I was a prize.

My hands relaxed as he kissed at my soft belly. It was no feat for him to yank the fabric from me. I stood before him in my disheveled bra and panties. The desire for him burned away at my self-consciousness.

Christopher knelt and pressed his mouth to the crotch of my panties. My knees buckled. He caught me, lifted me, and carried me to the bed. His perfect body came overtop of mine.

"I'm going to kiss you between your thighs," he said. "You can tell me no."

He spread my thighs until my heels reached the corners of the bed. I was trembling before he dipped his head. I watched the blonde tufts of hair shift as he cocked his head and looked up at me.

"Do you want me to stop, MK?" He hooked his fingers in the waistband of my panties and tugged. "What was that?"

"No. Please, no."

I knew what he was going to do. I wasn't so sweet that I didn't know the ways men and women pleasured each other. I'd imagined my husband-to-be going down on me, and me returning the favor. I'd just always assumed it would happen during my honeymoon, not after I'd watched a live sex show featuring two of my new friends.

When Christopher's lips struck my most intimate lips, I jackknifed off the bed. With the first stroke of his tongue, my hips moved of their own accord against his face.

"Fuck, that's sexy. Yeah, fuck my mouth, princess. Fuck, you taste so sweet."

My body undulated against his face as he flicked his tongue. The tight coil happened so fast, my eyes watered. I locked my legs over Christopher's back. I dug my fingers into the sheets. But the release wouldn't come.

As though he knew, Christopher reached up both hands. His face stayed buried in my core. Without looking up, his hands found the lacy edge of my bra. His fingers snuck under the fabric and found my nipples. All it took was a pinch of his thumbs and forefingers and the damn broke inside me.

A fingernail broke as I dug into the mattress. My ankles locked at Christopher's shoulder blades. Sometime later, Christopher made his way up my body and brought me into his arms. He held me tight as the tremors receded.

"So we're dating now?" he said.

FOURTEEN

"Whoops," said Christopher. "Looks like I dropped the soap... again."

He knelt down, filling his empty hands with my abdomen. Then my ass. Then my thighs. Christopher spread them apart like he was unwrapping a gift. Then he played with the treasures he found within.

The soap lay forgotten in the tub basin as he cleaned me up with his tongue. The sudsy water slurped down the drain mixing with the sounds of his lips against my core. His hands rose to my breasts. He found my nipples and gave them a pinch.

That was all it took.

Christopher stood and caught me before my

knees gave out. He held me and kissed me as the tremors stopped. Then he hefted me up and out of the tub.

I was too comatose to protest about my weight. My brain and virtue cried a warning. He was hard against my soft, wet flesh. It would've taken nothing for him to steal inside of me.

He'd let me put it in my mouth earlier this morning. It had been awkward at first until I looked up and saw the ecstasy on his face. The feel of him invading my jaws, sliding over my tongue, and spilling his essence down my throat transformed into something beautiful and sensual that I wanted to do again and again. In my mouth, and in other places.

I opened my legs and wrapped them around his waist. His penis behaved, aiming up instead of arrowing inside of me. I didn't hide my disappointment.

Christopher set me down on the bed and toweled me off. He paid particular attention to my breasts again. I felt the flutters rising within me.

"Careful, you're getting a little too excited, princess. We don't want to make a mistake."

I struggled to remember why that was a bad thing. Then I remembered our deal. We were dating.

Well, he was dating me. I'd already planned out our life together. In my mind, my belly was swollen with child number three. My mind would not let go of the idea that I was going to marry this man. It didn't matter that he didn't believe in the institution.

For Christopher, dating meant dinner, conversation, and kissing. Kissing anywhere on my body. We'd only been at it for a day. We'd had the house to ourselves. He'd made dinner. There'd been light conversation. But mostly, there was kissing.

"You are so sensitive." He pressed my thighs together, and then pressed a kiss to my lips. "I could play with you all day, princess. But I have to go to work."

"You won't be late. It's just a few steps from your house."

"No, my other job."

"Your mom won't mind if you're late," I said. "She likes me."

He stood and passed a grin over his shoulder before turning away from me. "I don't work at my mom's store."

I lay naked on this man's bed, in a house he shared with other men I didn't really know, and I had no idea how he spent his days.

As though sensing my confusion, Christopher came over to the bed. "I race cars."

"Like for NASCAR?"

He chuckled. "No. Street racing."

My brows furled. "Is that legal?"

He waggled his head. "Sometimes yes, sometimes no."

So that was that. The guy I'd mentally planned my life with, the guy I now had two kids with and was working on number three, that guy was a quasi-criminal. I didn't know what I'd tell the children. He wouldn't be able to go to Career Day at their elementary school.

"You're freaking out, aren't you?" He grasped both my hands and pulled me up until I was sitting before him. Now that I was leveled with his eyes, I saw that there was a speck of wariness there.

I reached up and ran my hand over his eyelids. He let me, turning his face into my fingers and pressing his lips into my palm. My heart squeezed as hard as my core had moments ago.

"I'm not freaking out," I said.

His lips quirked up. That mischievous grin told me he knew I wasn't telling him the whole truth.

Instead of owning up to it, I decided to change the conversation. "I'm just thinking about my own work. I'm having trouble with the middle of the book."

"Tell me. Maybe I can help." He went into his dresser and pulled a pair of jeans out of a drawer. He stepped into them. Commando.

I stood and pulled my bra and panties on. "The story is an ugly duckling trope."

He snorted as he put his arms into a button-up shirt. "You amaze me. I don't know how you write these things you know absolutely nothing about?"

I peered at him. He didn't appear to be joking. He truly didn't see how I didn't know the ugly duckling trope. How could I not be falling for this guy? I pulled my dress over my head and then continued the sketchy tale that was my steamy novel.

"The guy is popular and handsome," I said. "He approaches the heroine because of a joke. Then it turns out he needs her help. And then he starts to have feelings for her."

"I like it." Christopher came around the bed and buttoned up the back of my dress. "Let me guess what happens next. The friends and families get in the way of their love? They try to break them apart?"

I nodded. "They're from different worlds, so yes."

He turned me to face him. "I don't see what the problem is?"

"I'm in the middle of the story and it's sagging. I started off with a bang, but I've lost momentum. I can't figure out where to go next. If I go too fast, it might feel like I've missed all the details of why they fell in love. We call that the Fun and Games section in romance writing. If I go too slow, I risk getting too deep into the details and the readers will get bored and might put the book down."

"It sounds like racing," he said, putting his arms around me. "When you're at the starting line, there's always some jerk-off who revs his engine to show his balls are bigger. It gets attention. But if you rev too high before you take off, you can loose traction and the tires will spin out and you lose all power."

"So, how do you win?"

"You gotta pace yourself. You gotta know where the sweet spot is. And when you find it, you gotta take your foot off the brake and go full throttle. Wanna see? Come with me to the race."

FIFTEEN

There were women's booties everywhere that I looked. In threadbare skirts that were knit crochets. In Daisy Dukes riding up their crotches. In skirts I would bet were originally used as headbands. The women were all draped on cars like in the magazines. Or in men's laps like in porn videos.

"Hey Crow." A girl wearing a bright yellow bandanna over her ass sauntered over. "Want a tune-up before you get behind the wheel?"

Christopher grinned at her. "I'm good. My girlfriend took care me this morning."

The girl's eyebrows rose. I turned redder than the candy apple convertible parked beside us. I didn't know what shocked me most? That this girl publicly announced that she wanted sex? That

Christopher publicly announced that we'd been intimate this morning? Or that he called me his girlfriend.

Christopher pulled me into his side. He wrapped an arm around my shoulders and bussed my forehead. The girl shrugged and went to the next car and its driver.

"Stop playing footsie, Crow," Eagle shouted from across the way. "We got work to do."

Eagle's eyes landed on me before he ducked into the race car. Leaning against the hood of Crow's race car, I saw Ellie and Hawk kissing like no one was watching. Next to Ellie and Hawk, I saw a black woman and an Asian man leaning into each other.

Christopher brought me over to them. "MK, you know Eagle, Ellie, and Hawk. This is my other brother, Owl, and his girlfriend, Shakira."

Owl nodded, his dark eyes bright and welcoming.

Shakira looked me up and down. "I didn't believe it when Ellie told me Crow brought a girl home. You're nothing like I imagined."

I wasn't sure if I should be insulted? Shakira cocked her head to the side and continued to stare at me. She didn't frown. It was an assessment. I tried not to take it personally that the two African-American family members didn't take to me immediately.

"Don't worry, she said the same thing about me a few months ago." Ellie came around the car to join us.

"I told you then that Hawk would eat you up and spit you out," said Shakira. "I was half right."

The two women looked over at Hawk. Hawk winked at Shakira and blew Ellie a kiss. I looked at the two women and wondered if they shared their men. They stood together like they were friends, sisters from different mothers. The men laughed and joked like they were family. It was clear that not a single one of them shared parents.

"I know exactly what you're thinking, sis," said Shakira. "How are we cool if we're sharing dicks? I felt the same way at first. I've been cheated on by every man I've ever been with."

"So, now you're with a guy who does it in your face with your friend?" The words were out before I could take them back. Mercifully, neither girl looked upset.

"Not at first," said Shakira. "Owl and I broke up because I couldn't handle it."

"I don't believe all men cheat," said Ellie. "I have

fidelity and freedom in my relationship with Hawk. There's gender equality in poly relationships."

Is that what this was? I'd heard about polyamory. Mainly from television shows on cable. It was a religious thing. Mormons in Utah. Muslims in the Middle East. Even some countries in Africa.

"You do know that the guys are all polyamorous?" Ellie asked.

"No, they're not." Shakira sighed as though she were talking to a child. "They're all kinky freaks that like to fuck anything with a cunt."

She said it with exasperation, but there was no bite to her tone. Well, not much.

"Calling them polyamorous," Shakira continued, "implies they love and commit to all the women they fuck. Hawk loves Ellie and Owl loves me. I like fucking Hawk. Dude has a monster dick. And Eagle plays some wicked games."

Shakira glanced over at Eagle who was behind the wheel of Crow's car. Eagle caught her eye and licked his lips.

Owl looked between the two and chuckled. There was no jealousy in his gaze. He looked back at Shakira the same way my grandfather would gaze at my grandmother, like how Christopher looked at me the night he asked to date me.

I looked over to Christopher. He was bent under the hood beside Hawk. Another girl came over to them. Christopher smiled at her. She reached out and ran a hand down his bicep. He didn't remove it.

He'd said he liked sexual things I might never be ready for. Polyamory, open relationships, kinky sex, these were indeed things I might never be ready for.

I looked away from Christopher and into Shakira's watchful gaze. Her raised eyebrow said she knew this was too much for me and she was expecting me to bolt.

Ellie placed her hand on my shoulder. It was a friendly gesture. "You and Crow should talk about this," Ellie said. "Set boundaries."

I looked back at Christopher. He was shaking his head at the girl. She pouted and took off. He returned his attention to his engine.

"He said he wants to date me," I said.

Ellie nodded encouragingly. "Crow's a good guy. Funny, child-like, sometimes. Unfailingly honest, all the time."

That was good to know. But had I set any boundaries? Other than not breaking my hymen? We'd never clearly defined the boundary between his cock and other women. I hadn't told him that I'd already set a picket fence around us in my mind. That fence was the boundary I wanted someday.

I looked at Ellie. "Is this a fling for you? With Hawk? Or is this the real deal?"

Her eyes softened. "It's the real deal for me. It's true love."

I looked to Shakira. Her gaze was hard and sharp.

"That true love bullshit makes your pulse race and your heart pound," Shakira said. "Who wants that all the time? I'll take trust. Trust is a warm blanket on a cold night, like a dog. It doesn't let you down. Shit, listen to me."

"But don't you believe in soul mates?" I asked her. Didn't all women? That there was one person in the world meant solely for you.

Ellie nodded enthusiastically.

Shakira shrugged. "I can see myself spending the rest of my life with Owl."

"Hawk is my soul mate," said Ellie. "But even though he's my soul mate, I do enjoy having sex with other men. Not sex for sex's sake. I need a connection with someone to have sex."

Shakira nodded at Ellie's words as though she agreed.

I didn't know what to think of any of the words

they were saying. These looked like two confident, well-adjusted, beautiful women. But they let their men be with other women. They themselves were with other men. I didn't understand that.

"It's called compersion," said Ellie as though that was a real word.

Shakira rolled her eyes. "You got her totally in nerd-mode now. Buckle in. This may take a while."

Ellie ignored her. "Compersion is when a partner derives pleasure when the other receives sexual pleasure from another."

I couldn't imagine any pleasure in knowing that my boyfriend was having sex with another woman.

"Hawk has regular sex partners," said Ellie.

"Like Mrs. Robinson." Shakira said.

"That's not her real name. That's just what we call her. Mrs. Robinson likes it rough," Ellie explained. "Neither Kira nor I like that kind of stuff. So, the guys play rough with her."

"Don't you get jealous?" I asked.

"I do," said Shakira. "But that's just my nature. Owl knows I don't like being ignored. He gives me a lot of time and attention. And orgasms. It's hard to be mad when you're coming."

"No," Ellie said. "I don't get jealous of Hawk having sex with other women. I get jealous of the time he spends working on his car or hanging out with the guys. That's the type of quality time that I want with him."

Behind us, the engines roared. I turned to see Christopher behind the wheel of his car. He caught my eye and blew me a kiss before heading off to the start line.

A girl in hot pink booty shorts walked up to us. "There are the Watchers Crew sluts."

Shakira stepped in front of me. Her hands came to her hips in a defensive posture. "What's the matter? Sad you're not invited to the party?"

"Can I come to the party?" A guy came up to me. "I'd like to spread those sweet thighs."

He reached out to touch me. Before his hand made contact, I heard bones crack.

Hawk appeared out of nowhere. He engulfed the man's fingers in his huge paw. The man whimpered and then crumbled to the ground.

"Did you have permission to touch that piece of tail?"

I jerked back. It was like being slapped on both sides of my face. On the left side, from the brutality of Hawk's actions. On the right side, from the degrading words. I was not a piece of tail.

The man couldn't answer Hawk. He sobbed as bones continued to crunch.

"In some societies," continued Hawk, "you get your hand chopped off for touching what belongs to another man."

"Sorry," the man whimpered. "I'm sorry."

"Not to me, dip shit."

The man's eyes rose to mine. "Sorry. I didn't know."

"Now, you do." Hawk shoved the man away. "Don't ever touch my brother's property."

The man scrambled off.

I opened my mouth to deny that I was anyone's property. But the words were stifled by the truth. I wanted to belong to Christopher. I wanted to be his piece of tail.

I didn't want anyone else touching me. I didn't want anyone else touching him. I wanted to break off the finger of that woman who had touched his bicep before.

Hawk turned to me. "You okay, Mary Katherine?" He placed his thumb on my face, tilting up my cheek to check for bruises.

I forgot to flinch. His huge hands were softer than I expected. The rage seeped out of his hazel eyes and was replaced with concern as he checked me over. It reminded me of when I'd scraped a knee as a child and one of my grandparents fussed over me.

When Hawk saw I was unharmed, he let go of my chin. "Anybody bother you, you let me know."

He stared me down until I nodded. Then he turned and headed away.

Ellie came over and put an arm around me. "Sorry about that. Can't say it hasn't happened before."

I sat in the bleachers with Ellie and Shakira. They chatted me up, asking questions about my life, appearing genuinely interested. Ellie was genuine with her interest. Shakira still had an air of distance as though she was uncertain if I'd stick around.

The racers lined up below. I assumed that a street race would take place on the streets, but this was on an actual racing freeway. Ellie explained that this race was sanctioned, and that only Christopher was racing in it because he was the best at the rules. The other guys preferred the no holds barred aspect of illegal street racing.

I felt a twinge of pride at Christopher for being the best. I also didn't quite believe he was the straight-laced one of the bunch with the mischief always present in his eyes.

The engines revved. Just like Christopher had said, one guy revved high enough to have his tires smoke. A flag flew in the air. The lights changed from red to yellow to green. They were off.

The revving guy with the smoky tires spun out. A few cars jerked and sputtered before catching their gear. But Christopher's car rocketed forward. He was steady with three other cars.

They kept pace for a bit after the first curve. But somewhere approaching the middle of the track, Christopher gunned it. His car took a flying leap ahead of them. There was no way another would catch him. I leapt to my feet along with the rest of the crowd as he rounded the final bend of the track and more flags flew.

Christopher sailed into the pit in a plume of gravel and smoke. The boys of his crew pulled him out of the car, hugging and clapping his back in congratulations. A few girls surrounded him too. He smiled at each in turn, laughing; offering high fives, receiving hugs that lingered.

All the while his eyes darted left and right until he found me. His grin grew ten times bigger when he spotted me standing at the edge of the crowd. He made his way towards me, weaving between more bodies that offered more congratulations.

I could have made it easier by coming to him. But something inside me thrilled at him having to bypass all those long legs, choosing to ignore all those perky breasts, for him to brush aside those small waistlines, and come to me.

When he got to me, he caught me in his arms, sweeping me off my feet as though I weighed nothing. When he put me down I was breathless.

"Did you see, princess?" His voice was childlike as though he were a little leaguer who'd scored his first homerun.

"Of course I saw. My heart raced the whole time."

"I told you, it's all in how you start off." He pulled me back to him, molding my curves to his as easily as he'd taken his car around the track. He brought me in and kissed me like there was no one else for him in this crowd.

SIXTEEN

There were a lot of bodies crammed into the first floor of the Watchers' house. All but six of them were strangers to me. Hawk barbecued out on the back patio with Owl. Eagle, Kira, and Christopher mingled with the house guests in the living room. I helped Ellie serve food to the guests from the kitchen.

She pulled lasagna from the oven, but she told me she hadn't made it. Eagle had. I couldn't remember my father ever being in the kitchen. I could barely remember the last time my sister's husband sat at the dinner table with us. But the people who belonged to this house all pitched in.

Christopher kept a close eye on me. He found me every fifteen minutes or so. He'd sweep me away from the kitchen. He'd introduce me to someone new -always calling me his girlfriend. Always offering me a kiss before disappearing back into the crowd.

This could be my life. My husband, the racecar driver winning a race. Then coming home to celebrate with our friends and family. Only there wouldn't be couples making out at the dinner table. Or grinding in the moonlight off the back patio. Or stripping in the living room.

All around the room, conversation turned to kissing, dancing became groping, and clothing became optional.

I went to refill a bowl of chips and stumbled at the sight of two girls doing a striptease for Eagle. Eagle crooked a finger at one of the girls. The one who wasn't selected pouted but continued dancing seductively. To the other girl, the girl who had been selected, Eagle pointed at his crotch. The girl's eyes lit up. She reached down and unzipped his pants. My mouth watered at the familiar crack of the zipper's teeth.

"You enjoying yourself, Mary Katherine?"

I started as much at my full name on Eagle's lips as hearing his deep voice address me while he was getting a blow job.

"Crow says you have very sensitive breasts." He dug his fingers into the girl's scalp and yanked. A moan of protest dripped off her glistening lips.

Eagle's eyes took a long route down the V of my dress. I couldn't look away from the girl's tongue as she tried to get back at his cock. She completely ignored my timid gaze. The only audience she was interested in was Eagle.

"You should let me check that out sometimes." He rotated his hips, pushing his cock deep down the girl's throat. She squealed with delight. I saw her eyes close and her expression shift to total concentration before her hair fell into her face. She didn't swipe it out of the way.

"She's not into you." Kira came up behind me.

"Everyone's into me," Eagle said. His eyes held me in place as he thrust into the girl's eager mouth.

"Keep thinking that, asshole."

Eagle grinned. "I'll get into that asshole later."

"If you're lucky." Kira shoved her middle finger in his face.

With the girl still attached to his cock, Eagle lunged forward with his teeth. But missed as Kira hopped back. He settled back into the chair, undulating his hips into the girl's face.

It was the hunger in Kira's eyes that brought me

back to reality. Despite Kira's tough talk, I knew she loved Owl. And Owl's feelings for her couldn't be any clearer. I reminded myself that no one in this household considered sharing cheating. Even though Kira flipped Eagle off there had been a spark -no, a firework- of desire in her eyes.

I looked away from their flirtation to find Christopher. He stood before a girl that was unbuttoning her shirt. He looked down at her breasts and grinned like a kid who'd seen a long lost toy. Then he reached out and touched her breasts. His head canted to the side as though considering.

My stomach dropped.

His eyes looked up, searching the room until he found me. "Hey MK, you gotta come see this." He waved me over to the bare-chested woman.

Eagle watched me through heavy-lidded eyes as the girl on her knees continued to suck him off.

"You sure you want to be here, MK?" said Kira. I turned back to her. Her guard was down. Her eyes searched mine. "You don't have to do anything you don't want to do. You need to say exactly what you want. No one will think less of you if this isn't your thing, sis. But you'll regret it if you do something you don't believe in or something you're not ready for."

She took the bag of chips out of my hands and

went to refill the various bowls around the living room.

A hand came to my arm. "MK, come see," said Christopher. "She has a rosary tattoo, like your necklace. It's so cool."

I looked up at Christopher. There was excitement in his eyes at this new thing he wanted to tell me about, to share with me. It was just that the new thing was a woman's bare breasts.

Why couldn't it be a new book or a piece of artwork? The girl came over, her breasts on display. The ink on her chest was a piece of art.

Christopher reached out and lifted her left boob. "It's pretty, isn't it?"

"Yeah, that's lovely," I stammered. "You know, I'm a little tired. I'm thinking about heading home."

"Oh, no no no," he protested like a child being told his family was leaving the amusement park early. "Come upstairs and lay down in my bed for a while. I'll stay with you if you like?"

"But it's your party. I can't take you away from your guests."

"You're the only guest I want to be with." He put his arm around my shoulder, pulling me into his side.

I often wrote the cliché about how the heroine fit

perfectly into her hero. Her head into the nook of his chest. Her lips slanted against his. Her hand in his.

I never expected to fit in the cradle of someone's body. Christopher was tall and slim. I was of average height and overweight. But somehow my size-twelve hips fit perfectly into his slim waist. Locked into place at our hips, his arm wrapped tightly around my shoulder, we wove our way through the living room.

"Crow," said a girl who was completely naked. "We wanted to give you a victory fuck." It was one of the twins from the store. Pancake and her bottle-shaped sister sat naked in an armchair. "You can shoot your load on our breasts."

"Thanks, Chrissy and Fiona," he said. "But I'm spending the night with my girlfriend."

The girls turned their attention to me. "She can play, too," one of them said. I wasn't sure who was who.

Christopher shook his head. "It's not her scene. She's not into the group sex or exhibition sex thing. She likes one-on-one. You know, lovemaking."

There was no ridicule in his voice. Just truth. Part of me blushed at the bluntness of his characterization of me and my intimate preferences. But the other part of me warmed that he knew me, and my boundaries, and could articulate my needs better than I could.

Both Ellie and Kira had said that we needed to discuss our boundaries. But I didn't see a reason why if he knew my lines better than I did. He read my mind just like my heroes did in my books. He was my hero come to life.

"I'm going to take care of her needs tonight," he continued. "But we can play another time."

The girls agreed without protest and turned their attention to someone else.

I tripped up the step.

Christopher caught me in his arms. "You okay?"

My toe ached from being stubbed on the border of the stair step. A splinter went between the wedge of my pinky and ring fingers where I hit the wood of the step.

"Yeah," I said. "I'm fine."

Christopher led me to his room and shut the door. I heard the lock click behind us. Once we were inside, he brought me into his arms.

"I probably shouldn't have brought you here tonight," he said. "I had a feeling it would be too much for you."

I wanted to protest, but once again he'd voiced my truth. I remained quiet and snuggled into his chest. My head fit perfectly in the nook between his hard chest.

"These victory parties always devolve into sex orgies," he continued. "But I was selfish. I love watching you work and being a part of it. I wanted you to see me doing what I love, what I'm best at."

He took my hand in his. My hand fit perfectly into his palm.

"And then I wanted you beside me when I won. I wanted you in my arms more than any trophy. But I don't want you to be uncomfortable. Do you still want me to take you home?"

I heard the sounds of the party and the pleasure down below us. I understood why that girl looked disappointed when Eagle passed her over for her friend. I understood why the other girl's eyes lit up at being selected. She obviously knew what Eagle could do to her, just like I knew what Christopher could do to me.

This man held my heart. He'd held it the moment he asked me to tell him a story in his mother's sex shop. He'd collected any stray pieces when he unbuttoned my shirt in that back room and made me feel things I didn't know were possible with my breasts. Now, when he asked if I wanted to go home, my chest caved in in disappointment.

But it was a question, not a dismissal. He'd given me a choice. Christopher always gave me a choice.

I didn't drop to my knees and crawl to his crotch like one of the groupies downstairs. Instead my fingers went to the hem of my dress. I pulled it up and off. There was no cross on my nipple or tattoo on my breast. Only Christopher's hands. Each touch of his fingertips seared into my skin where they fell. His finger pads marked a circuitous path, branding my skin as his.

He looked at my breasts like the landscape of my chest was Heaven on Earth. He sat on the bed and pulled me down until I straddled his lap.

He brought my body forward. The first touch of his tongue was a long, reverent lick. It lasted for two seconds before he opened wide and swallowed me whole.

I flung my head back. He wrapped his arms around me, pitching my body forward. It brought my core in contact with his torso. The heat between our bodies was too much to bear.

Christopher swirled his tongue in exactly the way he knew would bring me to climax. But when I was at the precipice, he stopped. He shifted our bodies and flung me onto my back on the mattress.

Ellie and Kira had both said they didn't like rough sex, but I found being tossed around thrilling.

Christopher turned his attention to my core, pressing my thighs together. I protested. He chuckled as he wrapped his fingers around my panties and tugged them off. Then he spread my thighs wide. He gave me a wink before his head disappeared between my legs.

He wrapped my thighs around his shoulders. I flopped back on the bed and waited for oblivion. But then, something different happened.

Christopher's long licks reversed direction. He started at my clit, grazed my opening, and kept going. He kissed the small patch of skin between my core and my anus.

I squirmed as he got closer and closer to exit territory.

He gave my anus a tentative lick, and I bucked.

"Do you like that, princess?"

He didn't give me a chance to answer. He did it again.

I moaned deep in my throat. The sound rang in my ass.

Christopher reemerged overtop of me, a wicked light in his eyes. "You want to stay a virgin. That means no vaginal sex. What about anal?"

SEVENTEEN

I said yes. I can't believe I said yes. But I did and now Christopher was inserting a water bottle up my ass. It was a boundary I never thought anyone would cross. But he was there. Breaching this new frontier.

It was a squeeze bottle with a long neck that held some type of lubricant. The process reminded me of an enema. I tried not to think that, but I couldn't wrap my mind around this being in any way, shape, or form sexy.

"MK? Have you changed your mind?"

"Why would you think that?"

"Because you're tense."

"You have me in an awkward position."

I lay on my side on his bed with one knee drawn up so he could get to my ass.

Christopher was behind me, one hand rested on my hip. "This will be uncomfortable just for a second, and then I promise you'll see stars."

With just those words, my body responded. It relaxed and my sphincter let go of its grip. Warm water flooded into my ass. Instead of discomfort or embarrassment, I felt a warm flush spread through me.

"I need you to hold it for me, princess."

Christopher scooped me into his arms and carried me into the bathroom. My mind was suspended between holding the liquid inside of me and marveling that he didn't even break a sweat carrying my weight.

Once inside, he stood me back on my own two feet. When I turned to close the door, he moved past me, towards the sink.

"I'm sure you don't want to see this," I said.

"There's nothing you can do to turn me off. I find everything about you sexy." He leaned his perfect, naked body against the sink and waited patiently.

I looked between him and the toilet. This had to be the least sexy thing I could think of. In fact, I never would have imagined it.

"Sit down, Mary Katherine."

I sat down on the toilet obediently. I kept my knees pressed together. I stared down at the fleshy parts of my inner thighs and covered the fatty evidence with my hands.

Christopher knelt before me. He leaned my body forward. I felt the warm liquid jostling inside me. I clenched to keep it inside, mortified at the thought of letting it go with him in the room.

Christopher grinned and captured my lips. Once I was distracted, he spread my thighs. I lost the battle with the warm fluid when he reached down to play with my clit.

It was Christopher who cleaned me up afterwards. He washed his hands and then bent my torso over the sink. I looked at my reflection in the mirror. I was flushed, partly from embarrassment, mostly from arousal. The internal bath heightened my need to be filled.

Christopher pulled out an oblong tube from beneath the sink. "It's a butt plug. It will help get you ready for me. It's also another chance to see whether you think you'll like anal."

He lubed the plug. Then ran his fingers over my anus. I inhaled slowly at the pleasurable sensations. Then he aimed the plug up my sphincter.

"Just relax. Bear down."

I did, and it went in. I was surprised it didn't hurt. It also didn't feel pleasurable, just an overwhelming sense of fullness. He washed his hands again and then led me back to the bed. I waddled more than I walked with the obstruction in my back door.

He laid me down on my back. I felt the plug shift angles, and I winced. It didn't hurt. It was just not the most comfortable thing in the world.

Christopher opened another bottle and poured the oil on my belly. The liquid was cold, but when his fingers mixed with the oil, my skin heated. I forgot about the thing up my butt and focused on Christopher's hands roaming over my body.

He focused on my stomach for long moments, making me forget every self-conscious thought I'd ever had about my flab. He grazed my breasts, teasing me, before landing on my face. He massaged my face, running his fingertips over my eyelids. He massaged my temples. He leaned in and kissed my lips. Lightly, at first, but then more fervently.

Still kissing my lips, his hands traveled to my breasts. He circled my nipples in opposite directions as he sucked on my tongue. Once he had me whimpering, he took his lips to my breasts.

I was squirming before his tongue took its first

swipe of my nipples. The pressure rose. I pressed my thighs together but could only go so far with the plug stopping me from within. I pressed my ass into the sheets and my back arched up as my nipples hardened to painful points. The heaviness of my breasts weighted my chest down into the mattress.

I felt like I was pulled in different directions as the pressure rose. The orgasm slammed into my chest and swept through me. When it came to my core, the contractions met with the resistance of the plug in my butt, which made me clench harder.

"I will never get tired of that," Christopher said around a mouthful of my breast.

He flipped me over as the tremors subsided. He poured more oil on my back and massaged me there. I was near comatose with relaxation when I felt him part my ass cheeks.

He gave the plug a tug. My anus reflexively clenched as he pulled. It had felt uncomfortable when he'd placed it in there. It had multiplied the sensations when I reached my climax. Now that it was moving out of me, I found that there was something interesting in the feeling of the extraction.

With the plug gone, Christopher left me lying there. I heard him moving about but I felt too languid to take a peek at what he was doing. I heard the sound of foil. I heard the lapping sound of more oil being used. Then I felt him between my legs.

I gulped, my throat vibrating with uncertainty. The plug hadn't been all that pleasurable except when I came and then again when it was on its way out. I felt the head of Christopher's penis between my thighs.

"Just relax, princess."

He breached the skin of my anus and I gasped.

"I promise you, Mary Katherine. Trust me."

Christopher's penis was thicker than the plug. As he pushed in, there was a burning sensation.

"Bear down, princess. We're almost there."

He withdrew a bit. I took a shuddery breath. Again, the retraction of something coming out of my ass felt interesting. He thrust forward again and I grit my teeth.

He withdrew. I felt more oil drip on my skin. He massaged around my anus, keeping the tip of his cock in. I liked the massage. I didn't mind the tip of his cock at my back door.

When he thrust forward again, I tensed, grimacing before he'd moved a millimeter. But it didn't hurt this time. The burn was gone. There still was no pleasure. But there wasn't any pain.

He withdrew and there was that stimulating

feeling. I tried to wrap my brain around it. I didn't enjoy his thrusts. But with each retreat, I ached for his return.

He didn't withdraw as much this time. He thrust deeper, still slow, still in small increments. He made each withdrawal even slower than his forward thrusts. I focused on those delightful retreats.

Before I knew it he was fully seated inside my ass. I only knew it because I felt his balls brush against my swollen labia. I heard him struggle with his breathing. His fingers trembled as they rested against my belly. He rested his forehead against the back of my head and held still for a moment.

"Is everything okay?" I asked.

"You feel amazing," he whispered. "I don't want to hurt you."

"I'm okay. It doesn't hurt any more."

He inhaled. On his exhale, I felt him straighten. The hand on my belly went to my breasts. "I promised you stars."

He withdrew.

I moaned.

I felt myself clenching in my anus, as well as my empty channel, to hold onto him. I couldn't believe this was happening. I was having sex. And not any kind of sex I imagined myself having. It didn't matter where he'd entered. This man was inside my body, just as he was inside my heart.

Christopher methodically increased his speed. Before long the thrusts felt as good as the retreats. Better even, as he rolled his hips each time he filled me completely. That rolling of the hips was aimed at something deep within me. It hadn't quite reached the X yet, but each thrust put him closer and closer to the eye of the storm raging within. Until, with one wayward plunge inside of me, he hit the spot.

My eyes widened in alarm. I reached behind me to grab a handful of his skin to alert him. Something wasn't right. This wasn't that slow build of pleasure from all the other orgasms I'd had. This felt like a boulder, barreling straight for me, preparing to knock me over.

I was scared. Rationally, I knew it would feel good. But something told me it would be too much to handle.

My ears picked up sounds from birds chirping outside the closed window. My eyes spotted a tiny lint ball in the far corner of the room. I felt the sweat underneath my fingernails. I tasted blood from biting my lip. It was too much. I couldn't take it.

And I was right.

The orgasm knocked the air out of me. It

knocked the stiffness out of my bones. I collapsed onto the bed. It forced my eyes shut. I saw pinpricks of light that reminded me of the night's sky.

I lay in darkness as my body tried to work out the process of living again. Feeling came to my extremities first. I wiggled my toes and un-balled my fists. I took in slow, shallow breaths. Light danced on my eyelids. Soft, wet light that whispered a breeze.

Christopher pressed another kiss to my eyelids before I opened them. "No, princess. Go to sleep. I've got you."

He wrapped me in his arms. He entangled his legs with mine. He pressed his firm belly into my soft one. I felt a mess between my thighs; a mess of oils and sweat and cum, but I didn't care. I was ruined, and it was all for this man.

EIGHTEEN

It was early in the morning by the time the pleasure settled to a hum. I lay on my side and watched Christopher sleep peacefully. In his sleep, he reached for me and I came to him. It was automatic, an instinct. I was a piece in the puzzle of him. When I came into his arms, I heard the satisfying sound of all the groves and lines snapping me into place.

I watched his eyes open. When he saw my face he smiled. His lips found mine immediately. It was a light, lingering kiss. He was in no hurry to deepen it, or to end it. He simply sipped at me like I was his morning cup of coffee before a hard day's work.

"Can I see you tonight?" he asked. "Just to hold you. You'll probably be too sore for anything else.

Now that I've held you the past few nights, I can't imagine you not being there when I wake up."

I couldn't speak. My heart did an intricate swan dive and landed low in my belly with a sensational splash.

When I opened my mouth to verbally answer, his phone rang, beating me to a response.

He rose up on an elbow to peek at it. "It's the twins from last night," he said. "Let me text them that I'll see them later this afternoon."

My stomach grumbled audibly as he typed. "You're going to go see them? To service their cars or something?"

"No," he chuckled. "To service them. I'll see if Eagle wants to go too. I doubt I'll be able to handle the both of them after last night." He put his phone down and nuzzled into my cheek.

I tried to make myself comfortable in the me-shaped hole of his chest, but there was too much room now. The grooves didn't line up like before. The lines weren't exactly flush.

I could twist and contort my whole being. I could break myself into a million pieces. But I would never be able to cover every inch of his needs. I shifted out of his embrace and he let me go.

He watched me as I dressed. He leaned his

cheek against his arm and licked his lower lip as I pulled on my panties.

I was a prized piece to him, I knew that. I knew no other woman had the title he'd given me; girlfriend. I knew that no one else had a place in his bed. I knew that no one else felt his lips pressed against theirs.

I was special. I was unique. But I was still a piece in the puzzle of him. To me, he was the big picture.

"I love you," I said.

Christopher scratched at his heart. He opened his mouth, but no words came out.

"I don't think we should see each other anymore," I said.

He blinked so hard the crust of sleep fell from his eyes. "Why not? Did I hurt you?"

He was out of the bed lightening fast. His eyes and hands roamed my body looking for signs of damage. When he didn't find any on the surface, he peered into my eyes and searched my soul.

"I've done something wrong," he deduced, still peering into my eyes. He scanned them, searching hard to find the answers. "Is it because I didn't say *I love you* back?"

"I can't live my life in pieces."

"Mary Katherine, I don't understand what that means? I don't want you to be in pieces. I like you exactly the way you are. We didn't know each other two weeks ago. Now, I can't remember how I got by the days without talking to you. I can't remember how I fell asleep at night without holding you. Is that love? I don't know? I've never been in love. I've never felt anything like this before. Only with you. So...maybe?"

I tried to speak but my lips trembled. And then the tears fell.

"Oh no, no. Don't cry, princess. Love's not supposed to hurt. I know that much. I wouldn't have said it if I knew it'd make you unhappy."

"I'm not unhappy," I sobbed. "I'm just falling to pieces."

Christopher kissed the tears, my lips. "I don't know what I'm doing here, Mary Katherine. I never thought I'd ever feel this way. I never thought I'd find a girl who accepted me for who I am. I look at Ellie and Hawk and Kira and Owl, and I never thought something like that would happen to me. I always thought I'd just play around with a string of women until I was walking with a cane. But here you are."

I took a deep breath, burying my face in the space at his heart. "Yeah, here I am."

"I know you want to get married."

My entire being froze. Blood stopped pumping through my veins. My heart stopped beating. My lungs collapsed.

"Relax, princess," he chuckled. "I know it's way too soon to even think about something like that."

I tried to nod and agree, but my head wouldn't betray the truth. I'd already married this man in my head.

"I know our ideas of marriage, and relationships, and family are different. I grew up in an open family with a number of aunts and uncles who weren't blood relations. They were my parents' lovers. I'm sure your parents took vows to be with just each other and have stayed that way."

I didn't attempt to clarify the committed dysfunction that was my parents' union.

"I grew up knowing that what my parents had with each other was special," he continued. "I watched them welcome in other loves, and likes, and lusts. Those other people never threatened their bond. I think maybe I could have that with you. This is happening fast between us. I feel like I'm supposed to say let's take it slow, but I don't do things slow. Instead, let's just keep things at the same pace. Let's not slow down. Let's not speed up. Let's just be together. Okay?"

"Okay," I sighed and sank deeper into him.

"Let me splash some water on my balls and then I'll take you home."

He fit his lips against mine and at the same time rubbed a thumb over my nipple. I caved into him. I couldn't stop myself. It was automatic. It was instinct.

He pulled away and disappeared into the bathroom. I finished dressing in a daze. The buzzing of a phone pulled my eyes into focus. But it wasn't another booty call for Christopher. It was my mother calling on my phone.

I hit IGNORE. But as I did, an email notification popped up at the bottom of my screen. Needing the distraction, I opened the email app. It was from the school principal my mother had tried to set me up with. It looked like she wasn't done trying.

I starred at the bold subject line; A cup of coffee, it read. Up in the corner was his profile picture. He had a jovial smile, kind eyes, and an average body. He crouched in the midst of a group of kids. Everyone in the picture smiled in an open-mouth, frozen moment of joy. A part of me recognized that this was exactly the type of guy I would've been excited to date a month ago.

I looked up at the open bathroom door. I heard the water splashing and Christopher moving about. Christopher, my boyfriend who loved me. My boyfriend who would drop me off at home and then head out to be with not one but two other girls. My boyfriend who would do the deed with my full knowledge and then come hold me later tonight because he couldn't sleep without me in his arms. My boyfriend who'd put marriage on the table, far down the table, but it was there.

This was how he loved. Openly. Honestly.

I looked down at the unopened email.

Ellie said Hawk had rough sex with other girls because she didn't like it. Kira said her jealousy was curbed so long as Owl gave her orgasms and attention. Maybe if I had someone else filling my other needs, maybe then I wouldn't get jealous of other girls. Maybe then I'd understand this whole polyamory thing.

I opened the email.

NINETEEN

Christopher had slapped my ass many a time over the past couple of nights we'd slept together. Sometimes, when he was plunged so deep inside of me that I swore I would pass out with one more thrust, he'd strike my flesh with an open hand. Each time, it sent me reeling forward, only to come back to him for more.

Other times, he'd catch me in the process of getting dressed. He'd give me a playful thwack. That would then turn into a sensual caress. That would turn into needing to get dressed all over again an hour later.

I never pretended to be a dirty girl who liked spankings. I had no daddy issues whatsoever. I harbored no need to be punished or disciplined. But when Christopher got his hands on me, I'd melt into a puddle of wanton obedience and bow to his every whim.

Watching him spank another woman's ass left me cold and frozen in discontent.

"It fascinates me how thin the line is between pain and pleasure," Ellie said as we both watched the other woman get her brains bopped out.

"If Owl ever tried to choke me with his dick, I'd leave teeth marks." Kira rolled her eyes and turned away from the scene.

Inside the garage, the boys of the Watchers Crew were choking Mrs. Robinson. Not with their hands. First, Hawk shoved his cock into her mouth. Then Owl. It reminded me of an oil pump or a piston. Mrs. Robinson even gurgled up slick spittle as she tried to gobble them both down. Watching the display, my stomach turned and bile rose in my throat.

"They're not hurting her." Ellie assured me. "She likes it."

I couldn't see that. The older woman looked like she was in pain and distress.

"Watch her eyes," Ellie pointed. "They're pleasure glazed."

Mrs. Robinson's eyes were nearly black with arousal. Her eyelids looked too heavy to keep open.

"She's a pain slut," said Kira.

"I don't like that term," said Ellie.

"Bondage whore," Kira offered with a shrug.

"She's a submissive who finds pain and domination erotic," Ellie said. "She doesn't get it from her husband. So, she comes here and gets it from our guys."

Our guys. Even more sharing. I hadn't had to share this much since I was a kid. But there was my boyfriend, the man I loved, passing around a woman like she was a toy; a Barbie who liked having her limbs pulled in every direction.

"Does her husband know?" I asked.

"I doubt it." Ellie shook her head. "She should sit down and have a conversation with him. But I know first hand that not everybody understands deviant sexual needs."

Christopher took that moment to look up at the window. Ellie and Kira ducked out of sight. I stayed put. He locked eyes with me and smiled. He winked at me and then gave Mrs. Robinson another whack. The woman lurched forward.

I'd done the same thing when he'd spanked my ass last night. The spot still smarted. Instead of rubbing a hand over my backside to soothe it, I rubbed at my heart.

"I'm sure Mr. Robinson suspects his wife's having an affair," Kira said from her crouch beneath the window. "The woman's car is in the shop every other week. And she comes home with bruises all over her body."

"I won't shame another woman her kink. Everyone has the right to their own pleasure." Ellie smiled up at me as she hid under the windowsill.

"If your relationships with Hawk and Owl are open," I said looking down at the girls, "why are we out here hiding?"

Ellie stood up, brushing the dirt from her skirt. "I don't think Mrs. Robinson cares to have an audience. That's my thing," she grinned. "I also don't think Hawk likes me to see him like this; being rough."

"I don't particularly care to see Owl with another woman," said Kira as she retained her seat on the ground. "But I can appreciate another woman's orgasm after not having any of my own for so long."

Christopher looked at me again and smiled. I forced the corners of my lips to squeak upwards. I forced my eyes to keep watching.

He wasn't having sex with the woman. Well, not

exactly. He played with her breasts, slapping and pinching them. He'd never done anything like that to me. He played with my breasts every second he got, but he never pinched or hit them. I didn't think I'd like it. He knew me well enough to know I wouldn't.

Looking at Mrs. Robinson, she appeared to love it. She watched his hands with anticipation. When she could see, that is. Hawk's thick cock was jammed into her mouth. I saw where his cockhead landed as it pressed against the thin skin of her neck. Owl pumped inside her vagina. Eagle thrust up her ass.

I'd never seen a double penetration before. I couldn't imagine her husband being okay with this.

"More," Mrs. Robinson begged. "Harder."

"Are you telling me what to do?" Hawk growled.

"Please," she begged.

"Are you about to come?" he demanded.

It was clear that she was.

"Did I give you permission?"

"Please, Hawk, please."

"Not until I say so."

"Your boyfriend's an asshole," muttered Kira as she rose to standing.

Ellie grinned. "You know he's going to let her come. And when he does, it'll be even better. You know what it's like to wait for it."

A secret grin spread over Kira's face. I wasn't sure if the smile was a memory of Kira having sex with Hawk? Or her having sex with Owl? Though both couples were clearly in love with their respective partners, they made no secret that they enjoyed each other's partners.

I watched as Hawk made Mrs. Robinson beg for it. I saw the desperation in her eyes. I held my breath along with her in anticipation of her orgasm. Mrs. Robinson opened her cock-filled mouth and screamed her pleasure.

A hot furnace melted away the cold discontent I'd felt a few moments ago. My stomach did flips. I had to gulp several times as my mouth watered. Now, I couldn't look away.

Hawk moved away from Mrs. Robinson's head and came behind her. He motioned Eagle aside, but not out of her ass. Instead, he shoved himself inside her already stretched hole.

I gasped.

So did Ellie and Kira beside me.

"That's new," Kira breathed.

"Wow, the human body is an amazing thing," said Ellie as she licked her lips.

Four pairs of male eyes looked up at the three of us. They didn't look even slightly pissed. They looked hungry. Their eyes told us that this could be on the menu for any of us if we asked for it.

"Harder," Mrs. Robinson begged.

"Who told you to speak?" Hawk reached around and covered her mouth with his hand. He gave a signal to Christopher with his eyes. Christopher nodded and peered attentively into Mrs. Robinson's face as he continued to tug at her nipples.

I didn't blink again. I barely breathed. My heart pounded in my chest from the adrenalin of holding still.

Mrs. Robinson's moans were loud now. Christopher smiled down at her. He ran a gentle thumb over her nose. Something passed between them. It looked like permission. I knew because he'd given me that look on our first encounter. Christopher took his hand and pinched Mrs. Robinson's nose closed.

Mrs. Robinson's eyes rolled into the back of her head. Christopher watched her. He released his hold on her nose. She took a deep breath. Then he covered her nose again. He repeated this as the boys continued pounding into her. I saw her body trembling. Her pupils were impossibly large.

There was no love between any of the five people inside the garage. But they all took pleasure from each other. No one was faking it.

I felt a connection with the woman. Much like I'd felt when I'd watched Ellie come. I wanted Mrs. Robinson to come, just as much as she wanted it for herself. Everyone seemed to want it for her. Getting her there was a group effort.

So when she did come, I saw tension release from each male at their shared victory. I heard each of us women breathe a collective sigh of relief along with Mrs. Robinson. My eyes closed briefly, the first time they'd done so in long minutes. My heart slowed its gallop.

"Damn, that was beautiful," Ellie sighed.

The ride came to an end. The boys helped Mrs. Robinson put herself back together. They were incredibly gentle with her as they cleaned her up and put her clothes, and theirs, back on.

They chatted with her about her family and her car as they did so.

"Come on," said Kira tugging at my arm. "They're all going to be hungry after that work out. Owl made a quiche. Want some?"

I watched Kira and Ellie head back to the house. My feet stayed rooted to the ground beneath the window. I stood there trying to process what I'd just seen.

"Hey, princess." Christopher stood in the

doorway of the garage. He didn't come to me. He stood on the threshold smiling at me. The sun hit him and glistened off his blond hair.

I waited for outrage at what he'd just done. For jealousy. It didn't come.

"I was hanging out with Ellie and Kira," I said lamely.

"I love that you guys are cool. All my favorite people like each other."

Mrs. Robinson came out just then. She was put back together in a pair of black slacks, a pale blouse, and a blazer. She could've been my mother.

"Hey, Mrs. Pettigrew. I want you to meet my girlfriend, Mary Katherine."

Mrs. Pettigrew smiled at me. "Hello, dear."

"Hi." Now that she was put back together, I couldn't look directly at her.

"I need to hurry off," she said. "I have to pick up Dennis from soccer practice. I'll see you in a couple of weeks?"

"Sure thing, Mrs. P." Christopher turned his attention back to me as she walked away and got into her car. "She's good people."

"It doesn't bother you that she lies to her husband? That she's having an affair with you and the others?"

"Her relationship with her husband is between the two of them," he shrugged. "I'm glad she comes to us for her needs. Not everyone is trustworthy and some dipshit might take advantage of her or hurt her with the things she likes to do. If she told her husband... I don't know? Maybe he'd leave her? Maybe he'd take the kids away? Some people have good reasons to keep secrets. She says she loves him, I believe that. She shows him by taking care of his house, taking care of his family, by standing by his side. That's what love means to her."

"What does love mean to you?"

He smiled as he looked down at me. "It means another person's happiness is my happiness. Are you happy, princess?"

I took a step towards him, but he held up his hand.

"I've got another woman all over me. Let me take a shower before I touch you, okay?"

He blew me a kiss. It came to me on a light breeze. The sun shone on my cheek where his lips would have impacted. Warmth spread through my body. Contentment settled around my shoulders as we walked side by side.

I suppose that was happiness.

TWENTY

I didn't relish having dinner with my parents. Christopher had made love to me all afternoon and my ass disagreed with every chair it came in contact with. Every time my inner thighs closed around my clitoris, I had to spread them back apart. My breasts were too sensitive for my bra. All I wanted to do was go home and pull off all of my clothes.

But family dinners were an obligation. When I pulled up to my parents' house, there was another car in the driveway. It wasn't a car I recognized. The Ford Fusion was too sensible to belong to my sister's husband, who drove a two-seater Roadster that I'd only seen once parked next to my sister's Honda Odyssey.

Inside the house, my sister's children weren't

running amok. They each sat on the floor looking rapt at a youngish-looking man who sat before them in a chair making animated hand gestures. He looked up at me as I came into the doorway.

I instantly knew who he was. John Stafford, Principal of Central High. We hadn't found a time to meet in the last couple of days. Mainly, because I hadn't returned his calls. Truthfully, because my hands were constantly otherwise engaged down my boyfriend's pants.

Principal Stafford came up to me to a chorus of groans and whines from the children. My sister stepped in, eager to take his spot before her rapt children, but the children dispersed to opposite sides of the room before she reached the vacated chair.

"I'm sorry," Principal Stafford said. "I know what this must look like. I ran into your mother earlier this afternoon and she invited me over. She wouldn't take no for an answer. I assumed it was probably a set up and was ready to decline. Then she told me the dinner menu and there was no way I was backing out."

I giggled. He was funny, and non-threatening. Over my shoulder, my father gave me the thumbs up. I spied my mother in the kitchen picking out the good china.

My instinct was to pull Principal Stafford aside and tell him I was seeing someone else. That I was head over heels in love with someone else. Someone who had just fucked another woman in front of me this morning and then made love to me through the back door this afternoon. Principal Stafford would probably be scandalized and head out the door.

Instead of going there, I held my tongue. It was one family dinner. There would be plenty of other things to set him heading for the door soon enough. If my father didn't overwhelm him, or if my sister's kids didn't scare him off, or if he didn't catch my mother's cold front, and he still wanted to see me after all of that? Well, then I'd know there was something wrong with him, and I'd be the one running out the door.

Besides, he was right. It smelled delicious in the kitchen. My mother had outdone herself. She sat a plate of roast chicken and green beans in front of me. I noted that on everyone else's plate there were potatoes. I opened my mouth to protest, but decided to save myself the argument.

I wasn't hungry. I'd eaten plenty at lunch with Christopher this afternoon. He'd pushed a second helping on my plate, watching me with hunger in his eyes as I took in every morsel offered.

Never once had he looked at my body with disdain as I caught my mother doing out the side of her eye. Never once did he signal me to suck it in and sit up straight. I dressed in my cutest, most flattering outfits every time I went to see him. If anything, Christopher preferred me flat on my back with all of my flesh rolling and bouncing around. I'd never felt more beautiful and comfortable in my own skin than I had these past weeks with him.

Over dinner, it was apparent that John Stafford would have been the exact type of guy I would have dated. He ticked every check mark; educated, kind, loved kids, and he even went to church on Sundays.

"Did you know there's a contemporary religious art showcase that opens this weekend?" he said. "Would you like to go with me, Mary Katherine?"

I did want to go. And I wouldn't mind going with him. I doubted Christopher would be interested in religious art. Aside from the rosary tattoo on that random woman's breast, we'd never broached the topic of art. Aside from my rosary, we'd never again broached the topic of religion.

John was excited to see the works of a Japanese artist who infused abstract expressionism with the traditional art of Nihonga. I didn't know what that meant but I wanted to see it. My excitement grew with the way his eyes lit up and his hands waved around excitedly. I sat as captivated as my niece and nephews as he spoke about it. I nearly whined when my mother cleared the dishes away signaling the end of dinner.

John walked me out to my car. As he opened my car door, he asked me again to accompany him to the exhibit.

I was in an open relationship. There was no reason I couldn't go with him. It wasn't like I was going to sleep with this guy.

I declined the invitation.

With a sad smile and no explanation, I got in my car and pulled away from my parents' house. The truth was, *I* wasn't in an open relationship. *I* was a one-man kind of woman.

I couldn't see myself being with anyone other than Christopher. I couldn't imagine that another man could make me feel the way he did. I was all in. And I wanted him to be all in too.

I pulled up to my complex. Through the window, I saw Christopher sitting on the hood of his car. He grinned when I pulled into my spot. As I cut the engine, he came to my door to hand me out.

"Where've you been?" He pulled me into his

arms, running his hands up and down my back as he pressed me into him. "I thought you'd be writing."

There was a part of me that wanted to sass him. To tell him I had a life outside of my writing desk. Outside of his bed. That I had other men interested in me. But a wave of guilt swept over me.

It was irrational that wave. I'd watched him in an orgy with another woman. All I'd done was have a conversation with another man. And that man hadn't even touched me.

"I missed you," Christopher breathed into my hair.

I melted. Of course I melted. This man simply needed to look at me and I was reduced to a puddle. "You saw me this afternoon."

"Am I turning into one of those clingy boyfriends?" He pulled away looking sheepish. "I'm sorry. I guess I didn't get my fill of you today."

"You filled me up pretty nicely."

"Yeah, I did" he smirked. "I just want to hold you now. I've had a long day, and I just want my girl in my arms."

I stopped my brain from wondering if work or pleasure had caused his day to be long. It didn't matter. He was here now.

There had only been one night that we'd spent

apart since I'd first slept in his bed. He had traveled for a race a few nights ago. He'd called me that night after the dust had settled. Then he arrived on my doorstep the first thing the next morning.

"Is that okay, MK? You know you can tell me to beat it if I'm crowding you."

"It's not too much. It's perfect."

He smiled, running his hands through my hair and loosening the barrette that held my ponytail. "By the way, my mother wants you to come over to meet everyone."

"You want me to meet your family?"

"Of course, I do. Unless that's too much, too soon? I'm still not sure how all this commitment stuff works."

"No, it's not too much. It's..." I couldn't speak past the fluttering of my heart, which choked my throat.

"Hey, princess?"

"Yeah, Christopher?"

"Are you sore? I could kiss it better."

TWENTY-ONE

I don't know what I expected walking into Christopher's parents' house. Nude art on the wall? Grown folks fornicating in the corners? A sex swing?

The neighborhood we pulled into could have been my parents' neighborhood. It was early afternoon and we were stopping by for lunch. Inside the house, there was a riot of colors. Completely unlike my parents' museum-style house that was shades of beige.

Christopher's mother came up and hugged me the moment I stepped over the threshold. I couldn't remember the last time my own mother hugged me.

"You look lovely, Mary Katherine."

"Thank you, Mrs-"

She shook her head. A tinkle of laughter spilled from her mouth. It was like Christopher's laugh. "You did tell her this was a house of heathens. It's just Holly, dear. Come meet the rest of the family."

The introductions made my head spin. There was Holly's life partner, Christopher's father, whose name was Terry. There was Holly's boyfriend and his wife. There was also Terry's lover, who was a man, and his wife, who happened to be Holly's best friend. I could not keep all the names or connections straight.

"Confused?" Christopher whispered into my ear.

"Yes," I breathed.

"Freaked out?"

I opened my mouth to deny it, but nothing came forth.

He chuckled and pressed a kiss to my temple.

We moved deeper into the house where a man rolled on the floor with children. Christopher released my waist and dove into the fray. The kids chanted Uncle Christopher and attacked.

"Hi, you must be Mary Katherine." I looked at the blonde woman who approached me. "I'm Susan, Chris's sister."

I offered my hand; Susan came in for a hug.

"That's my husband, Scott," she pointed to the man on the floor in the fray of children. "And those are all my rug rats." She ticked each child off by name. There were four of them. "You have no idea how long I've waited to meet you."

"We've only been dating a couple of weeks," I said.

"Yes, but I've been waiting for years for my baby brother to find love. Trust me, if he brought you here, to show you all our family's crazy, his feelings run deep."

I looked down at Christopher. It was the first time I'd seen him with children, outside of my imagination. I had never seen my sister's husband play with his children. I'd never experienced my own father at play. I'd always gone to my grandparents' for any affection. Christopher looked like he was in heaven on the floor with the kids. My ovaries pulsed.

As the men and children played, Susan took the opportunity to tell me every embarrassing story she could remember about Christopher. I listened and watched Christopher give piggyback rides.

On the walls were a mountain of pictures; Holly, Terry, and three blond-headed children at various stages of life, in different locales, with a host of people surrounding them. Christopher had told me that his brother was traveling overseas.

"You have a large family," I said.

"My mother doesn't let anyone go. It's like the mafia; once you're in you can't get out. Every boyfriend, girlfriend, lover, playmate is still apart of our lives, even if they aren't intimate with my parents any longer. Holly is very big on family."

"You call your mother by her name?"

"Most of the time. She doesn't like labels. She's an anarchist. But don't call her that. I was anarchical growing up. I believed that if you labeled one person, it devalued another. Then I met Scott and I haven't felt the need for anyone else."

"You two are legally married?"

Susan nodded.

"What did you say in your wedding vows?" I asked.

"We pledged our lives to each other, promised to face challenges and to nurture each other as we continued to grow. We promised to be loving and faithful partners. We've kept every one of those promises."

Scott looked up at her then. He winked and blew her a kiss.

"I still consider myself poly," Susan said. "He knows I would never cheat on him. I'd come to him if I developed feelings for another soul."

Holly came in to announce that lunch was ready. Dining was a communal affair. Holly and Terry served Ethiopian food with spongy bread, lentils, and veggies that everyone ate with their hands.

Everyone told stories about Christopher to embarrass him -and they all knew stories. His father told stories about him in little league. His mother's boyfriend told stories about taking Christopher and his older brother fishing. Even his mother's lover had stories to tell.

Through all the laughter and joviality, I forgot who was attached to whom. As dishes cleared, they accepted me in, treating me as a part of the family. I even got charged with a chore after the meal.

I stood next to Holly drying off the dishes she pulled from the sudsy sink. "Can I ask you something?" I said.

"How do I make all of this work?" she guessed.

I smiled at her perceptiveness. "My mother and sister have trouble managing just one relationship. I've never even had a boyfriend before. With Christopher, I feel like I'm being asked to fly before

I've learned to walk. I don't want to fall on my face."

"You definitely are a writer, aren't you," Holly said with a grin so like her son's. "I don't believe one person can be everything to you. I think it's a lot of responsibility and pressure to expect of a single person. I need different things in my life, so I collect different people. I wanted children, and I chose Terry to partner with in that endeavor. I knew we'd make good co-parents and life-partners. I love to travel, but Terry's a homebody. So, my boyfriend Pat, his wife, and I all travel together. Terry's bisexual. He fell in love with Corey when we were in college. But Corey wanted to stay in the closet. He married Lily and suppressed his feelings until a few years ago when he came out. Terry and I supported them both through it and the men fell in love all over again."

Up until now I'd only worried about Christopher with other girls. Now I had to wonder if he was into guys, too?

"It's a lot of work managing all these relationships," Holly said. "But it's enriched my life."

"I get jealous," I admitted, running the dishtowel over the tines of a fork. "I see him with other women and I get jealous."

Holly nodded. "Jealousy is a natural human trait. What you need to ask yourself is where is the jealousy stemming from?"

"I feel that if he's allowed to have these other choices, he'll find someone he likes better." I put the last of the dishes on the drying rack.

"You think that limiting his choices will keep him by your side?"

"That sounds awful when you put it like that."

Holly smiled. "Those are your feelings, and they're valid. But it's not likely how Christopher feels. He hasn't stopped talking about you since you came into the shop. He's never talked with me about any of his relationships. I think you just might be special to him." She said the last phrase in a singsong voice.

Something settled in my soul, but there was still an itch in my heart. "I feel like I'll never be enough for him."

Holly leaned her hip against the counter and tilted her head, considering. "I think love changes over time, but it's always there. My love for Christopher's father has done that; it's changed over the years we've been together. He's had partners that were different from me, and I had feelings of inadequacy. But those were my feelings. It didn't mean he loved me any less, or that he was prepared to leave me for another. We brought those people into our lives. I've made a life commitment to Terry, and he's made one to me. Even when we're pissed the hell off at each other, we would never go back on that promise we made to be there for each other no matter what."

"How is that any different than a traditional marriage?"

"There's an exit clause called divorce," Holly chuckled. "Irreconcilable differences, infidelity, incompatibility, these are all a natural part of human existence, as well. They're likely to happen over the course of a relationship. People use those excuses to walk away. Don't do that. Walking away is so damned easy. Staying and working things out, that's harder."

Holly pulled me into her arms and I came.

She rubbed my back just like my grandmother used to do.

"Talk to Christopher," she said as she let me go. "Tell him how you feel. Otherwise, you'll fall into the trap of hoping he figures it out and solves it for you, and that won't happen. Two heads are better than one. Three and four are even better. And if you don't know how to talk to him, you can talk to your girlfriends. Ellie and Shakira are lovely girls with good heads on their shoulders. And you can always come and talk to me. No topics are off bounds. You're apart of the family now. When I collect people I don't let them go."

TWENTY-TWO

On the drive back to my place, my belly was full and my heart was light. But the gears in my head were turning. I was going to talk with Christopher about my jealousy issues. Though they seemed insignificant now when he twined his fingers with mine and pressed his lips to my knuckles.

I knew he didn't have feelings for Mrs. Robinson, or the bopsy twins, or any of the other girls he had sex with. They weren't the woman he loved. I was.

What was there to be jealous of? He always made time for me. As soon as I thought to miss him, he'd call or text or come over. When I was with him, I had his full attention. Even if he had another woman's breast in his hand, he still looked out for me.

Should I even bother him with any of this? Was it a big deal?

It was my issue. Not his.

We pulled up to my place. Christopher cut the engine. He leaned over and kissed me. "Let me walk you inside."

"You're not coming in?"

He shook his head. "I've gotta handle something with the guys." He unbuckled his seat belt. He looked up and smiled at the disappointment on my face. "It shouldn't take too long. I'll be back tonight."

He got out and opened the door for me, taking my hand. It was that time of the day that was after noon but before evening. The sun was still visible on the horizon, but the bright orb was sinking fast. Storm clouds moved in and muted its rays.

"Are you guys playing with other women?" I asked.

Christopher wrapped his arm around my shoulder and tucked me into his side, right in the spot where I fit him so perfectly. "I don't know? Maybe?"

Now is the perfect time to say something, Mary Katherine. Don't expect him to read your-

"Do you have a problem with me playing with random women?"

His mother, Ellie, Kira, they were all wrong. Christopher always knew exactly what I was thinking, exactly what I needed.

"Kira doesn't like it when she doesn't know the girls Owl plays with," he said. "They agreed he'd only play with girls she knew or girls that came to the parties at the house. Is that something you want?"

I remembered Kira crouching on the ground outside the garage when Mrs. Robinson came over to play. She'd said she didn't like watching Owl play with others. But then she'd stood next to me and watched the boys bring Mrs. Robinson to a shattering climax. We'd both sighed as we'd felt the aftershock of that climax.

Thinking back on it now, it didn't really bother me that Christopher had played around with Mrs. Robinson. He clearly didn't have feelings for her, and neither did she for him. It had been fun for them both. And if I was honest, I kind of enjoyed watching it. Way more than when I'd tried to watch the online and DVD porn. What happened with Mrs. Robinson had been real, not fake. Like with Ellie and Hawk.

"We can talk about it when I get back. I won't be long, I promise." Christopher let me into my place using my key. He paused in the doorframe and smiled at me. "You know, I really thought my family would freak you out, and you'd turn and run. I was nervous about that."

I stood rooted to the spot in my foyer. He reached out and ran his hand over my rosary. His fingers counted the beads that rested over my heart. It had a calming effect on us both.

"I don't want you to run away from me," he said. "I want you to stay."

I reached my hand out to the small table where I kept my mail. "You should take this."

"Is this your spare key?"

I shook my head. "It's your key, for whenever you want to come over and stay."

He captured the key in his hand and my mouth with his lips. He pocketed the key, stepped out, and shut the door behind him.

For the next half hour I tried to focus on my work, but I couldn't. My heart was light, cushioned in a cocoon that knew it was love. But my mind wouldn't rest. It wanted to focus on any and every-thing except my manuscript, which was a problem because my deadline was looming large. I needed a distraction to wrangle my muse.

I looked at the clock to see it was only 4:30pm. Next to the clock was a postcard from the local art museum that featured the contemporary religious works that Principal Stafford and I had talked about. It was just the distraction I needed.

There was only an hour left until the doors to the exhibit closed when I got there. I walked the halls looking for meaning in the water-colored angels, collages of scriptures, and expressionistic renderings of prophets. I wondered what Christopher would think about the Fall of Man installation that used a recycled tire as the skin for the serpent. I'd like to believe he would've humored me and come along, but I doubted he'd actually enjoy himself here.

"Mary Katherine?"

I turned and saw John Stafford standing next to an expressionistic painting portraying the Temptation of Eve.

"It looks like great minds think alike," he said as he walked up. "Do you mind if I join you?"

I was about to say no, but then I thought of Holly and her boyfriend who she traveled with because her life partner liked to stay home. I thought of Hawk who liked rough sex from time to time, but always treated Ellie with love and care. I liked art and literature and foreign movies. I suspected that my boyfriend wouldn't care for any of those, just like I didn't care for racecars, video games, or Adult Swim.

I remembered how much I liked my conversation with John. He was fun, in an academic and brainy kind of way. There wouldn't be any harm in hanging out with him at this exhibit. I wasn't about to give him my spare key. Nor did I think of him as a potential lover. I didn't want another lover. I wasn't built that way. But I wouldn't mind a new friend.

John was truly engrossed with the exhibit. We walked the halls together, stopping and discussing each painting in turn. John was just as insightful and engaging to talk with as he'd been at dinner. He interpreted one painting of Jesus on the cross with an army of birds flying out of his back as the death of the *Old Testament* and the birth of *The Book of Revelations*. I thought it was about forgiveness.

In a portrait of Jesus in a boxing ring with gloves, which I interpreted as turning the other cheek, John found metaphors in the bloodstained wrappings on the prophet's hands and the name written across his boxing shorts that read *savior*. With each painting and sculpture he encouraged me to think deeper. It was exactly the distraction I needed. My mind shoved aside the writer's block and creative thoughts sprang forth.

We stood staring at an abstract painting of the Mother Mary for long moments without speaking. I turned to him with a thought to see that he wasn't staring at the painting. He was staring at me.

I knew that look. It was full of interest and desire. When his eyes caught mine, they asked if I felt the same? Disappointment settled all around the creative wellspring in my head. It looked like this friendship would be over before it had ever truly began.

Before I could set John straight, I heard someone calling my name. I looked down the hall to see Ellie. Her eyes flickered to John, whose eyes were still glued to me. I stepped away from him and toward Ellie.

"Hey, Ellie," I said embracing her and then bringing her between John and me. "This is my friend, Ellie. Ellie this is John Stafford. He's... a friend."

"It's nice to meet any friend of Mary Katherine's." Ellie shook John's hand.

There was an awkward silence as we stood next to a sculpture of Mary Magdalene.

"Will you excuse me for a moment, ladies?" John said. "I'll be back in a second, Mary Katherine." He rested his hand on my lower back before taking off in the direction of the men's room.

I looked at Ellie. "I didn't know you liked religious artwork. I would've invited you. John and I are just friends. Well, not exactly friends." The words all tumbled out of my mouth in a jumble.

"You don't have to explain all of your relationships to me, MK," she said. "All that matters is that Crow is cool with it."

I stood stiff as a board, as though a cross was on my back. Why did I feel guilty? I hadn't done anything wrong.

"But it's fine if he doesn't know," said Ellie. "That is, if you guys have decided on a more anarchical relationship?"

I didn't know what that meant? "I'm not in any relationship with John. We'd talked about coming here when we had dinner with my parents."

Ellie arched an eyebrow at the last statement. But then she reached out and gave me a squeeze. "Mary Katherine, you don't have to explain any of this to me. I'm not going to judge. But if you need to talk about anything, you can call me. Okay?"

"I think I do need to talk about... a lot of things."

"Okay." She gave my hand another squeeze. "Why don't you come over for dinner tomorrow? I'm baking pie."

"I'd like that."

John came back at that moment and Ellie took her leave. I was no longer excited to see the rest of the exhibit and tried to beg off. He insisted on walking me to my car.

"I had a good time," he said as we reached the parking lot.

"I did to." And I had until he took an interest in me instead of the art. Much like he was doing now. "Listen, I-"

John's lips crashed into mine. It surprised me, which was why I didn't push away immediately. Before I could tell him to stop, he pulled away with a grin.

"That was probably a little forward of me," he said.

"It was. It was very forward."

"No, I understand. That was too soon. I can take a step back. We can go slower. But Mary Katherine, I think there is something between us."

"No," I said. "There isn't. I don't have the same type of feelings for you. I thought we could be friends, but I was wrong. If you feel something, and I don't, we can't be friends. I'm going to go."

I got in my car before he could protest.

TWENTY-THREE

"I'm all for women's liberation," Christopher said around his fork. "But I'd keep you locked in a kitchen with the way you bake, El."

Ellie giggled and served him another helping of her pie. I was too busy unbuttoning the top of my jeans to feel an ounce of jealousy. He was right. Ellie was a master with an oven. She said it all came down to science. A recipe, she insisted, was a procedure. And she was good at following procedures.

Around the table, everyone shared stories of their day. Hawk and Eagle groaned about a particularly tricky car repair. I chatted with Ellie and Owl about a book we had all read. Kira and Christopher chatted about a television show they were both watching.

And then the conversations changed. Hawk and Kira argued over a super hero comic book. Owl and Christopher discussed mufflers. Ellie got up and went into the kitchen.

Eagle turned to me. "So, Mary Katherine?"

I waited, but he didn't complete the sentence. Tonight showed me that everyone accepted me into this circle. Except Eagle.

"Yes, Eagle?" I cocked my head and studied him as he studied me. "What's your real name, by the way?"

"Privileged information. So, you write chick lit?"

"I write romance novels that explore female empowerment and the ideals of love in today's society."

Eagle's eyes sparkled, like I'd thrown down a gauntlet. "I like assertive females. A woman who knows her own mind, who knows what she wants, and goes after it, is damn sexy."

"Then we should get along."

Eagle grinned, holding my gaze, but he didn't respond. I wasn't sure if I'd passed his test or not? I decided I wasn't going to win this staring contest. I got up and went into the kitchen to help Ellie.

"You having a good time?" she asked.

"Yeah," I said. "Everyone's so great. You guys are like a family."

"We are a family. The bonds I made with these people are stronger than those with my blood family could ever be."

"Ellie, I wanted to talk to you about what you saw the other day. That guy... It was..."

"You don't have to explain."

"But I don't want you to think poorly of me."

"I don't." Ellie reached out for my hand. "You're trying to figure all of this out, I can see that. I was just as confused when I started seeing Hawk. In fact, I already had a boyfriend."

"John was never my boyfriend. It wasn't even a date. We bumped into each other and he got the wrong idea. I love Christopher. I only want to be with Christopher."

"Then that's what you should do." Ellie said it like it was that simple.

She placed a tray of drinks in my hand. We brought the drinks back to the table. Everyone had finished their slice of pie. One piece was left. The boys tapped out. Ellie and Kira looked at me. I wasn't interested. I'd need to spend the next month working these carbs off. I put my napkin on the table in surrender.

Ellie and Kira faced off.

"We could split it," Ellie offered.

Kira scoffed. "It's barely enough for one of us."

"I have an idea," said Eagle. "Let's have a little contest. Winner gets the treat."

"What kind of contest?" Kira raised an eyebrow. But it was clear to see that she was on board with whatever Eagle was about to suggest.

Eagle got up and disappeared into the living room. When he came back he held two pink, metallic eggs in his hands. Both orbs were attached to wires and rectangular joysticks.

"A coming contest." Eagle turned the nob on one of the joysticks. The egg came to life and buzzed. "First one to blow loses."

"Fine," said Kira as she looked at Owl with a winning grin.

"Wait, no," said Ellie. "They can't be partners. He'll just command her not to come for an hour."

I sat up straight. Was that possible?

"You take Hawk and I'll take Owl," Ellie said. "That'll make it fair."

"Fine," said Kira.

The two women stood and changed partners.

"Here are the rules." Eagle handed each man an egg. "Vibrators only. Fingers are allowed, but no mouths or tongues. We've all made you come before so we can tell if you blow. But you girls are on the honor system."

They cleared a space on the table. Ellie and Kira both removed their bottoms and panties like this was normal. I looked to Christopher. He chuckled as he wrapped his arm over the back of my chair.

"My money's on Shakira," he whispered in my ear. "Owl likes to control her orgasms. It's Hawk's goal in life to make Ellie come as much and as hard as possible."

Both of my new girlfriends climbed onto the dinner table and spread their thighs for their friend's boyfriends. Hawk immediately got to work.

"Fuck, Hawk," said Kira.

Hawk chuckled as he pinched Kira's clitoris. When she threw her head back, he rolled the bud between his thumb and forefinger. I saw his machinations clearly because both Kira and Ellie were clean shaven. Looking at the helpless expression on Kira's face, and listening to her moaning gasps, I agreed with Christopher. Kira was about to lose.

Glancing over at the other pair, Ellie's eyes were on Kira's face. She had an arm behind her head, resting her cheek above her armpit while she watched the ecstasy play across her friend's face.

Down below, Owl made slow circles on Ellie's inner thighs.

"Holy, shit," Kira panted.

Hawk's fingers moved lightening fast over her clit while he pressed the egg just inside her core. The buzzing from the vibrator sent shivers down my spine. Kira's legs shook as she let out a defeated, pleasure-glazed groan.

"Fuck you," she groaned as the tremors took her.

"Maybe after my girl gets her piece of pie." Hawk put his slick thumb in his mouth and winked at her. Then he turned his attention to Owl. "You better finish her off, man."

"Of course," Owl smiled. "Can I borrow that?" He indicated the vibrator that was still inside of his girlfriend.

Hawk gave it a tug that sent Kira through another round of shivers.

Owl took the proffered device and put it on Ellie's clitoris.

Ellie's hands, which had been behind her head, came down to the table where she gripped the edge. Her thighs fell open and her eyes closed.

Owl began a rotating motion, like a massage, with the two eggs. He circled her clitoris, never landing directly on top of it.

A low moan left Ellie's lips. Hawk stared at her, rapt. I caught Kira's gaze as she sat up. Gone was the sting of defeat. Her lip curled in a mischievous tilt as she watched her boyfriend at play.

Owl's hands moved over Ellie, slow and methodical. It reminded me of a magician waving a wand over his hat. He didn't say *Abracadabra*, but there was magic at work.

A wave rolled through Ellie's body. It began at her feet. Her toes flexed and then pointed. Her knees bent and her hips rose. Then her torso pressed down into the table and her chest rose. Her head tilted back and her mouth opened. The sound of her moans filled the room.

Hawk sat back in his chair, completely enraptured at the sight.

Christopher's fingers went through my hair. "That was beautiful, wasn't it?"

If I could speak, I would have to agree with him. It wasn't love between Ellie and Owl, or Kira and Hawk. It was crystal clear who belonged to whom. But at the same time, every person in this group had a hand on the other. A hand of support. A hand of guidance. A hand of encouragement. And a hand in their pleasure.

The last wave of pleasure rolled through Ellie,

but Owl's hands didn't stop with their magic act. They continued until he achieved a hat trick and pulled a second and then third orgasm out of Ellie. Her entire body shook so hard that the table legs squeaked on the floor.

Owl took the vibrators off her clit and out of her core. Ellie lay motionless. Hawk scooped her up from the table and cradled her in his arms.

Owl picked up the plate with the solitary piece of pie. "Here's your pie, Els."

Ellie didn't even open her eyes to respond. She turned her face into Hawk's chest and whimpered.

Owl turned to Kira. "Here you go, babe."

Kira climbed into her boyfriend's lap and ate the pie that he fed her with his fingers; fingers that had been all over another woman. Kira ate every last bite of the pie and licked Owl's fingers.

"Speaking of coming..."

I startled at the sound of Eagle's voice. I'd forgotten he was even in the room. He turned his gaze to me.

"I hear you can come just from having your breasts touched, MK? Is that true?"

"You've already had your fun for the night, Eagle," said Owl.

"I would be a bad host if I didn't make sure every woman in my household had a good time," he said.

"Don't worry, brother," said Christopher. "I'll take care of her."

"I'm sure you will. I was just curious if this was an isolated phenomenon with you, or if she could do it with another guy?"

"You know this reverse psychology bullshit only works on co-eds?" said Christopher.

"Leave her alone, E," said Hawk. "She's not into the group thing. Or maybe she's just not into you."

They all laughed, but Eagle's eyes continued to challenge me. I was never one for peer pressure. I'd been on the outside of the popular clique in high school and college I was able to see each of these manipulations for what they were. But this was something else. It felt like an invitation into this family.

Everyone else in this room had accepted me. One of them loved me. Two of them counted me as friends. And the other two guys had placed me under their wings of protection.

But this guy?

"Hawk's right," I said. "I'm not into you."

Eagle's eyes sparkled as though it was the answer he expected from me.

My hand went to unbutton my shirt. "I doubt you could get any kind of rise out of me."

Eagle's eyes widened in surprise. The room went quiet as I exposed my bra. Christopher turned to me with an eyebrow raised. I already knew I only liked Christopher's touch. I doubted Eagle could even make my nipples pebble, and I wanted to prove it.

The top of my shirt hung open, and all eyes were on me. I tried to hide my gulp, but Eagle caught it.

He held up his hands. "What does she like, bro? Soft? Hard? Real hard?"

I knew he was both asking Christopher's permission to touch me and also giving me a last chance to back out.

"Don't help him," I said to Christopher.

Christopher chuckled and rested back in the chair. His arm lightly touched my shoulder, letting me know he was there.

I watched Eagle's fingers as they came closer and closer to my chest. He had long, slender fingers. His brown digits contrasted starkly with my pale-skin and pink bra.

I looked down to see my chest heaving. Each inhale brought my breasts closer to his fingers, which had stopped mid air. I looked up to catch him watching me with a glint in his eyes, studying my reaction.

This was a game to him. Just like with Ellie and Kira. And just like with Ellie and Kira, I realized that there would be no loser. Eagle won the moment I flicked open the first button of my shirt.

I didn't have feelings of love for Eagle. I wasn't even sure I liked him. But what he did to me felt really, really good.

I gulped and pressed my knees together. His grin spread and he winked at me. His hands landed on the lace of my bra, light as a feather. There was no pressure needed.

My eyes flicked around the room at all the eyes looking at me. Something heavy spread throughout my chest. It wasn't embarrassment or self-consciousness. There was no judgment on any face. Only curiosity and interest and awe.

"That's so cool," Ellie said as she peeked out from the cradle of Hawk's thick arms.

I gripped the arms of the chair as my chest heaved. The fullness spread southward, and I knew that an orgasm was eminent. I made the mistake of looking into Christopher's face. There was joy shinning bright in his blue eyes as he looked between his friend's hands on my breasts and my face.

"God, you're beautiful," he said.

"Yeah, she is, bro," said Eagle.

Other murmurs of consent filled my ears. I closed my eyes as the orgasm crested. And then everything went black.

TWENTY-FOUR

When I opened my eyes I was in Christopher's bed, wrapped in his arms. "What happened?"

"You passed out." He pressed a kiss to my forehead.

I closed my eyes and felt the flush sweep over my skin. "I'm so embarrassed."

"Don't be." Christopher ran his fingers through my hair and pressed a kiss to my temple. "Everyone thought you were beautiful. Ellie's determined to have a breastgasm. You can probably hear her trying if you listen closely."

I did. Ellie and Hawk's bedroom wasn't that far down the hall. I wasn't sure if she was having an orgasm from her breasts being manipulated, but she was definitely having an orgasm from some place on her body being explored.

"Mary Katherine," Christopher whispered, his forefinger rubbed at my lower lip. He opened his mouth. Then closed it. Then he laughed. "You make me happy. I want you to know that."

I lay on my back, surprised that I could fall any further for this guy. But I did.

"When we met, I told you I wasn't a prince," he said. "You make me want to go out and slay a dragon, princess."

I nudged Christopher's arm off my torso and stood. I pulled my blouse, still partly open, over my head. Christopher lounged back and watched my striptease with a small smile on his handsome face.

"I don't need any dragons slain." I shimmied out of my jeans. Then my bra and panties. I crawled onto the bed, naked, open. I reached for the man I loved and placed his hands between my thighs.

His grin slipped. For the first time since I'd known this man, a serious expression spread across his face.

"MK?"

"I'm ready."

Christopher pulled his hand back. "Mary Katherine..."

"I'm sure, Christopher. I love you. I'm not built to fall in and out of love. This is it for me; you are it for me. I see myself spending the rest of my life with you."

I thought he might bolt out of bed, but he didn't. He pushed a strand of hair out of my eyes.

"I understand," he said. "I just want everything to be perfect for you, like in one of your books. I can light candles. I can run out and grab roses to put on the bed. You should at least have music. Don't you want music?"

I crashed my lips into his. "I have everything I need right here."

Christopher pulled me into his lap. His lips began a slow exploration of my mouth. He kissed me until I was dizzy. He ran his hands through my hair. My thighs spread wide and wrapped over his crossed legs.

His lips made a slow path down to my breasts. He looked up at me as he suckled my nipple. With one hand he rocked my hips into his, teasing me with his patience.

"I've waited all my life for you, Christopher. Please don't make me wait any longer."

He stood and made quick work of his clothes. He grabbed a condom and rolled it on his firm erection. When he returned to me on the bed, he picked up his snail's pace once again.

"I thought you liked speed," I whined.

He chuckled. "Don't rush me. This is a big moment for me. Taking the innocence of the woman I love."

"That ship sailed the day I met you."

He came to kneel between my thighs. "I love you, princess."

"I love you, too."

He lined himself up with my entrance. I took in a deep breath, but not as deep as his. He pressed inside me, just the thick head that I'd felt before in my mouth and in my ass.

It felt different as it slid through my folds. We always went slowly when Christopher entered me from behind. I didn't expect there would be much resistance from this end, but there was.

That same sense of invasion and tightness assaulted me. Unlike with anal sex, I didn't want to wait for it to pass. I wanted to be filled. I ached for it.

And then, it was all gone.

"Holy shit, MK," he said as he yanked himself out of me.

"What? What did I do wrong?"

Christopher's breath came in pants. His upper

body shook. Down below, I saw the dark pink head of his penis throb. "Oh princess, you didn't do anything wrong. But I was about to."

"Christopher, I want this."

"I do, too. But I was one stroke away from being a selfish bastard. Fuck you're tight."

He took in another breath. I reached for him, pulling him to me. He caved easily on shaky limbs.

"I don't need fireworks and crashing waves," I said. "At least not this time."

He shook his head. "You deserve tsunamis and rockets and earthquakes every time, princess."

He kissed me. His length throbbed as it stroked up and down my folds. He reached his hand down between our bodies. I felt his firm length move over my hipbone, slide past my clitoris, dip between my folds, and breach my entrance. I widened my hips to let him in. He hesitated at the door again.

He took in another deep breath, let it go with a shudder, and pushed further in.

"Oh god, Mary Katherine."

He took another breath, and with another shudder, he slid further in.

"Holy Christ, baby."

Another breath. I felt his stomach tremble against mine.

"Hari Krishna, princess."

With a gust of breath, he was inside of me. He rose above me. His lips quivered. His eyes glistened.

"I'm not going to last." His voice shook on a whisper as he spoke.

I pulled him down to me for a kiss. I moved my hips up to meet his. His body caved into me as mine had done the first time he'd touched my breasts.

We moved in unison. Christopher clutched at me, holding on for dear life. He shook his head from side to side, his eyes wide in wonder. He moved slowly, carefully. His teeth grit together. I could tell he was losing his hold on his climax.

I reached up and pinched my nipples. He looked down at my fingers. A chuckle broke through his shaking chest.

"Fuck, I love you," he said.

I pinched my nipples harder. It didn't take much. With him buried inside of me, and his love raining down on me, I felt the swelling deep inside of me. He felt it too because the smile melted off his face and the pained ecstasy returned.

I'm not sure who fired first. But my core clenched, and his erection released, and we came, together, in unison.

TWENTY-FIVE

The sun streamed in on my face, but that's not what woke me the next morning. It was Christopher. He planted light butterfly kisses on my eyelids. My eyes opened immediately because my reality was better than any dream I'd ever had.

"Good morning," he said.

I groaned in agreement. The smile on my lips was as big as the orgasm that had sent me into slumber. Christopher captured my lips in one of his slow, leisurely kisses that said he had all the time in the world and he wanted to spend it with me.

"I never thought there was a difference between fucking and making love." He slid his fingertips across my temple, displacing the baby hairs at my crown. "I was wrong."

My voice was still nowhere to be found. I gave over my mouth, my body, my thoughts to this man with an angelic face and a devilish glint in his clear, blue eyes. He looked at me as if I were his own personal slice of heaven.

With one more lingering kiss, he rolled off me and out of the bed. "What are you doing today?" he asked.

If the question were directed at my body, the answer would've been staying in his bed and replaying the acts of the previous night. But the businesswoman in me overruled that idea.

"I've got to finish the end of the book," I said.

I was so close to being done. My characters had already passed the All Is Lost moment where my heroine, believing herself in love, learns about the bet that initially brought my hero to her door. The hero was left alone in the Dark Night of the Soul moment as he realized he was well and truly in love and wants to spend the rest of his life with this amazing woman.

All that was left was to get them back together with a Grand Gesture. That was the part of the book that I excelled at. But I was having trouble in this story. None of the words in the big speech from my hero were resonating.

"Can I do anything to help?" Christopher leaned over me, a sensual glint in his eyes as he nipped at my nose.

"You've done enough." I lifted my head for a proper kiss. "I can figure this part out on my own."

"I've got to run out for a minute. Why don't you hop in the shower? When I get back, I'll take you home so you can get to work. Then I'll come to your place this evening and make a romantic dinner after your day of hard work."

"That sounds lovely."

He disappeared into the bathroom, came out fully dressed, and left before I'd finished wiping the sleep from my eyes. I took a long, leisurely shower and pulled on yesterday's clothes. Instead of wearing my top, I pulled one of his shirts out of the drawer and slid it over my head. I felt wrapped up in this man head to toe, inside and out.

I came down the stairs to a quiet house. There was shuffling around in the kitchen. Assuming it was Ellie, I went in.

It wasn't her cooking over the stove.

"Morning, MK. Want some pancakes?"

Eagle had a spatula in his hand, low-slung jeans on his hips, and nothing else. I stopped in the doorway. My mind flashed back to the other night with him kneeling before me with my breasts in his hands.

He raised an eyebrow as though he read my mind. I expected his eyes to dip to my breasts, but they didn't. He held my gaze. He leaned his hip against the stove and waited to see which move I decided to make.

"Yes," I said coming into the room. "Thank you."

Eagle nodded his head in approval, and then turned back to the pan.

My unease at being alone with him dissipated as my nostrils filled with the sweet smells of whatever was in the pan. I took a closer look. In one pan were fluffy, golden pancakes. In another-

"Are those crepes?"

"Yup." He maneuvered one out of the pan and onto a plate. "But, the pancakes will be up in a minute."

"Oh," I couldn't hide my disappointment. "I like crepes."

He appraised me anew. "No one else likes them. Too fancy for this burgers and fries crew." He picked up the plate of crepes and handed it to me.

I took it from him greedily. The first bite melted in my mouth and I groaned.

"Another satisfied customer," he purred.

I narrowed my eyes at him, but I didn't set my fork down. After the second bite, I said, "I love, Christopher."

He flipped a pancake. "I figured."

"I don't want to have sex with you."

"I figured." He glanced over his shoulder at me. His head cocked to the side and his eyebrow arched. "Do you think that's a requirement to be apart of this family?"

"I...?" I didn't know?

Eagle brought a second crepe over to my plate. He uncapped the syrup and poured it on. Way more than I had for the first crepe, which was exactly how I liked it.

"We're alike, you and me," he said. "We both like to watch pleasure. Real pleasure. Not the fake shit online or in videos. Right?"

My mouth fell open. But then I closed it.

"I don't need to fuck you to get you off. So, we're good." He winked and turned back to the stove.

I opened my mouth to retort, but what could I say? The Internet porn didn't arouse me. Watching Ellie and Hawk, and then Ellie and Owl, and Kira and Hawk, and even Mrs. Robinson, did. If I was honest with myself, I had liked watching those live scenes play out. They aroused me nearly as much as having Christopher's hands on my body.

I turned my attention to the second crepe when Owl and Hawk came in to the back door.

"Good morning, MK." Owl bent and kissed the top of my head. "Sleep well?"

I didn't have a chance to answer. Hawk pulled up a chair on the other side of me. "MK, you're a writer. Do you think you can help me with this ad for the shop?"

"I... sure. I can take a look at it."

"Cool," he said. He stared at the crepes on my plate. "You know you don't have to eat that shit. I can make you some pancakes."

"No." I pulled my plate towards me. "I like it."

Eagle chuckled from the stove. Hawk shrugged, distaste written all over his face.

"Hey, MK," said Owl as he refilled my glass of orange juice. "I was looking for a new book to read. I'm a huge fan of historical, literary fiction. Do you have any recommendations?"

Eagle shoved another crepe on my plate. Hawk pulled up the ad copy. Owl and I compared To-Be-Read lists.

By the time Christopher returned, my belly was full thanks to Eagle. My fingertips were blue with ink as Hawk and I rewrote his ad. And my already bursting TBR pile was now doubled from Owl's suggestions.

I fell asleep in Christopher's car as we made our way to my place. I awakened like I did this morning; to butterfly kisses on my eyelids.

"You hungry, princess?"

I groaned and held my bread-bloated belly.

"Well then," he shook his head with mock sadness, "I guess we'll just have to work up a sweat."

"I can barely move," I giggled.

"Don't worry. I'll do all the work." He came around the car and opened the door. He pulled me out and into his arms.

I thread my fingers through his hair and brought his lips to mine.

"Mary Katherine?"

I looked over and saw Principal John Stafford frowning at the two of us. In that moment, I felt like I was in the principal's office. I pulled away from Christopher. "What are you doing here?"

"I thought maybe I came on too strong on our date. I was going to offer to take things slower, but…"

He trailed off, waving his hands to indicate the lack of space between Christopher and I.

An irrational wave of guilt swept over me. Until I realized, I hadn't led this man on. I had expressed my disinterest the first night, and then again outside the museum.

"This is my boyfriend," I said. "The reason I'm not interested in dating you."

"You never told me you had a boyfriend when I asked you out."

Christopher stepped aside so he could look into my face. "You were dating this guy?"

"No... well, not exactly. We had dinner at my parents' house."

Christopher took another step back.

"My parents set that up," I said. "And then we bumped into each other at the museum."

"And you kissed me," said John.

"No, you kissed me," I said.

"You let him kiss you?" asked Christopher. His lips parted as he stared down at me.

My head spun from the three directions this story was being stretched. I focused on the most important part.

I stepped back and wagged my finger at Christopher. "There is absolutely no way you are going to make me out to be the bad guy here. I didn't sleep with him. I didn't even come close to it. How many women have you been with since we've been together?"

Principal Stafford balked. "Mary Katherine, you are not the woman I thought you were. Dating more than one man at a time. Sleeping with multiple part-ners -and out of wedlock." He shook his head and backed away. I was surprised he didn't make the sign of the cross as he went.

"You let him kiss you?" Christopher repeated. His voice sounded small.

"I..."

He shook his head at me. Was this seriously happening?

"If I'd pursued another woman, the way I pursued you," he said, "kissing her, taking her to meet my family, sleeping with her -actually sleeping with her where I held her through the night, how would you feel?"

I could only shake my head and hands. It was not the same thing. "So if I had just fucked him, that would be okay with you? If I'd let him play with my breasts, that would be cool? Or is it that I didn't have your permission? That you didn't know? Is that how this works?"

He didn't say anything. His jaw tensed. He turned away from me and stormed back to his car. He left me standing there. He slammed himself inside and took off going zero to sixty in ten seconds.

TWENTY-SIX

Sunday night dinner was not the place I wanted to be. But I'd been reminded in the past few weeks that family was a place of solace; a place of comfort or consolation in a time of distress or sadness.

"I spoke to Principal Stafford," said my mother. "I can't believe your behavior, Mary Katherine."

My mind flashed back to Holly and her tribe. I could picture her now, relying on her community to help her do mundane things like the dishes. I saw her planning future events with her boyfriend and his wife. She'd make sure she spent quality time with each and every family member and ensure they had what they needed from her.

"We didn't raise you to be like this," said my father. "Dating two men at the same time."

I wrapped my arms around myself as Owl had done to me the other day before I left with Christopher. Hawk had given me a cheerful farewell while Eagle looked on with an open smile. I'd felt like I belonged in a place I'd never expected to fit.

"It's those romance novels," my sister piped in. "If you think slutty behavior, at some point, you'll act on it."

I thought of Christopher's nieces and nephews. They were being raised in a village of people they could turn to at every corner. So unlike my sister who pushed away any attempt at help, certain only she could do things right.

"Louisa Mae, watch your language," said my mother.

"Mary Katherine's in the wrong, not me."

"You slept with a married man," I said.

"Mary Katherine watch your tongue," said my father.

"You're a married man sleeping with other women," I said.

"I will not have that kind of talk in my house," said my mother.

I looked around the room at the collection of aghast faces in the light of the truth. Denial was a dark front moving quickly over their expressions. I would receive no support from within these walls. These people had never ensured I had what I needed. Each person in my family was only out for themselves.

It was why I'd spent so much time with my grandparents when I was younger. Holly had said walking away was so easy. She was right. Staying was hard. Coming home after weekends with my grandparents was always hard. Sitting still at family dinners while I was starving for food and positive attention was hard.

Getting up and walking out of my parents' house was the easiest thing I'd ever done. I may not have been an expert on real love, but I knew it shouldn't hurt or shame the receiver.

Each member of my family had taken vows; thick and thin, better or worse, rich and poor. Each member of my family had let go of their end of those bargains.

I left my family's home with thick tears in my eyes, feeling worse for the wear, and poor in spirit. No one came after me. I didn't expect them to.

. . .

"YOU'LL HAVE to rework this ending, Mary Katherine."

The next morning was the start of the workweek. After leaving my parents' house, I'd spent all Sunday night writing and finishing my manuscript. I shuffled the phone to the other ear as I listened to Moira.

"The HEA is completely glossed over," she said. "There's barely any emotion there. I don't believe these two will make it."

I sighed, running my fingers through my tangled hair. I hadn't brushed it since yesterday.

"Let me guess," said Moira. "You broke up with your boyfriend?"

Christopher hadn't called or texted or stopped over since leaving me Saturday night. I felt the loss acutely. I couldn't sleep. Instead, I'd finished the manuscript and sent it over to Moira early this morning. It was late afternoon now.

"See, this is why I don't do relationships. When I need my urges met, I go to a bar, have a one-night stand, and never see the guy again. Men are bastards. Who wants to keep one around all the time?"

And this was the person in charge of feeding women's romance addictions. But maybe she had a point. I'd written all my previous books without a relationship, lost in the fantasy of what an HEA could be. I was in the after now and it sucked.

My doorbell rang. I got off the phone with Moira, making promises to flesh out the ending with more emotion. I opened the door and Ellie and Kira poured in. Ellie enveloped me in a hug. Kira went for my fridge.

"What are you guys doing here?" I asked.

"Crow said you had a fight. He wouldn't give any details."

"That still doesn't explain why you're here. You're his friends," I said. "Shouldn't you be with him?"

"We're family," Ellie said.

"Plus, he didn't come home last night," said Kira.

My heart cracked wide open. Of course he didn't come home. He was laid up with another woman, or two, or more.

"And we're on your side -obviously." Kira took a tub of ice cream out of my freezer.

"There are no sides in a family," Ellie insisted.

Kira rolled her eyes. She came over with three spoons and passed them around. "Whatever he did, he was wrong."

"He was an ass," I agreed. "But I didn't disclose

something and I should have. I don't think he trusts me any more. So, it's over."

They both frowned.

"You're giving up too easily, MK," said Ellie.

"She's right," agreed Kira. "If you love him, you need to fight for him."

My own family had practically disowned me. Now, here were these women I'd known for less than a month taking time out of their day to console me. I didn't know what would happen with me and Christopher, but I wanted to keep these women in my life. I hoped I got to keep Hawk and Owl too, and maybe even Eagle, if Christopher and I couldn't work things out.

Did I even want to work things out? I wasn't sure? I wondered what he wanted? Was he even thinking about me? Or was he on top of some other woman consoling himself right now?

I dug into the tub of ice cream with my friends. They let me man bash for a while. Once I'd exhausted myself, Ellie shone the light of reason.

"You both put too much into this relationship to just let it go," she said. "You can keep being pissed for awhile, but eventually, you'll need to talk to each other. And I mean really talk. Don't just say what you think he wants to hear. Tell him your whole truth. The good, bad, and ugly of it."

TWENTY-SEVEN

Twenty-Seven

I STARED AT MY MANUSCRIPT. There were words on the page, but I knew the words would satisfy neither my editor nor my readers. This story simply didn't have a happy ending. The hero was a jerk and the heroine... she was a push over. She was nothing like my other female leads. Those women were strong and assertive. They didn't put up with any funny business from their men. And the men all swooned at their feet and then swept the women off theirs. But not this heroine.

She didn't stand up for herself. She didn't put up

a fight when the hero did things she didn't like. She was a total push over. She was me.

I closed my laptop and stood. It was dark now. Kira and Ellie had left hours ago after offering a sleepover. I'd declined knowing I had to put some more work into this book. But they'd promised to come by tomorrow for a girl's night out.

Last night, sleeping without Christopher, I hadn't gotten an ounce of rest. I was sure I'd have the same issues tonight. He'd become ingrained in my life after such a short time, so much that I craved having his arms around me. I ached to hear his voice, his laugh. I wanted him to look at me with those soft blue eyes. I didn't need the sex. I just wanted him.

I wondered where he was right now. Was he with another girl? Was he trying to replace me in his heart? I knew I would never replace him in mine.

I walked over to the window. I looked down at the street and saw a familiar car. It was his. He sat in it with his head in his hands. He leaned his head back, looking up at the sky. There was pain on his face. My every instinct told me to go to him, to comfort him.

He reached for the door handle. He paused. But then he got out. He made his way to the apartment building.

I raced to the bathroom to brush my hair. I'd been in the same underwear since yesterday. I ripped it off and splashed water between my legs. Then I froze.

What the hell was I doing? Was I about to allow myself to be pushed over again? I didn't put my underwear back on, but I did pull a new attitude over me.

I wondered if he'd use his key and barge in. But this was Christopher. He knocked. My feet rooted.

He knocked again. The knock wasn't demanding. Christopher had never demanded anything of me. He'd always asked, with a smile.

He knocked a third time.

I opened the door.

His eyes raked over me, taking their time. I held still. His gaze came to my breasts. I wasn't wearing a bra.

Finally, he reached my eyes. "Hey," he said.

"Hey," I mimicked.

"Can I come in?"

I hesitated.

He held up his hands. "I just want to talk."

I stepped aside and let him in. It looked like he was in the same clothes as he'd been wearing the last time I saw him. He hadn't even been home. He'd been out all night with another woman, or more. My heart plummeted to the floor.

I still had my hand on the door. "Christopher, I've changed my mind."

He turned, eyebrow raised.

"I can't let you in. I can't do this again. It hurts too much."

He came to me. His arms on my shoulders. His eyes full of concern. "What hurts?"

"You going out and sleeping with anything with a skirt when you get mad at me. You broke up with me because I was out with another guy, but you've been out sleeping around since yesterday."

"Wait a minute, MK." He shut the door and leaned against it. "You just said a lot of things. I'm going to address the most important one first." He took a deep breath. "Who the hell said we broke up?"

My mouth slackened. I had to rotate my jaw before the words could form. "You left me Saturday night."

"Yes. I left. Because I was jealous. I've never felt that, and I didn't know how to handle it. I've never felt possessive of something before. I've never been in love."

He raised his arms as though he wanted to bring

me into them. Then he let them fall back down to his sides.

"You hurt my feelings," he said.

"*Your* feelings?"

He shook his head and sighed. "My mother was right about us."

I'd felt relief when I'd left my mother's house the other day, but the thought of Holly dismissing me was more than I could bear.

"We need better communication," he continued. "We both keep assuming the other knows how we feel, what we want, what we don't want. Neither one of us are mind readers like in those romance novels where the hero and heroine just know what the other is feeling."

I tried to focus on his words, but they jumbled in my head. The next words out of his mouth rang true and clear.

"I love you," he said. "For me, those words, that feeling, means I've made a commitment to you. I'm not going to break it, or break up with you, just because I'm mad."

He walked into the living room and took a seat on the couch. He looked back up at me and shrugged. "I'm not going anywhere. I'm all in. And we're going to sit and talk this through."

I wanted to go to him, to curl up in his lap. But I couldn't. I couldn't go through this again the next time we had an argument. "And then the next time you get mad, you'll just leave for a night and soothe yourself with anything with two breasts."

He stood and came to me. "I spent the night at my mom's."

"Oh."

"You should know that I'm a bit of a mama's boy. Apparently, I have attachment disorder, which means that once I find something I like, I don't let go."

He wrapped his hand around mine.

"My mom told me I was wrong for not talking this through with you. She said you were wrong too, by the way."

"Me?"

"We both need to define the parameters of our relationship. The fact that we love each other isn't enough. We need to quantify it, as Ellie would say, so we get better quality. It's become clear to me that you're not comfortable with me playing with other women."

"I'm sorry, but it's not. It makes me feel insecure. It makes me jealous."

He nodded, but then he frowned. "Even when

you know that you're the only woman I love? The one I want to spend my life with?"

"But don't you know that about me, and my feelings for you? You still got jealous."

"Because I didn't know about that guy. If you want to date him, I can be open to that. But I need to get to know him, too, if he's going to be with my girl."

My jaw hit the floor. "Why doesn't that bother you?"

"I told you." He wrapped his arms around me. "I'm not going anywhere. This is my spot. This is where I belong."

"I don't want to date anyone else."

"Okay. I won't play with anyone else either. Not until you're comfortable with it."

"And if I never get comfortable?"

He inhaled and sighed. It wasn't an annoyed sigh. It was contemplative. "I love you more than I need to go out and play with other women."

I melted into his body. I wrapped myself around him, secure that I would never let go, for better or worse, rich or poor, through thick and thin.

"Maybe someday we won't want a physical relationship," he said. "Maybe you'll choose to have children with someone else, or live with someone else.

That won't ever stop you from being a part of my family, a part of me."

"I want to make it official," I said. "I want you to marry me. Not because I don't have faith in your word. Because I want the right to sue you if you ever tried to walk away from me."

"If it'll make you happy." He grinned with the devilish glint in his eyes. "Your happiness is as important as my own. On most days, it's more important."

He pressed his lips to mine, softly, then firmly. He drank from my lips like a man who hadn't taken a drink in days. He lifted me off my feet and carried me to the bedroom.

"Can we do the talking thing in the morning?" he asked.

"Sure. We've got a lifetime."

EPILOGUE

The house was alive with celebration. As always, people were peeling off clothes after crossing the threshold of the front door. It was a joint celebration. Christopher had won his race earlier this afternoon. And earlier this morning, my steamy new release had hit number one in New Adult Erotic Romance on Amazon.

I was already hard at work on a new title. The sex scenes were getting easier and easier to write. I drew a lot of inspiration from the bopsy twins, Chrissy and Fiona. My newest heroine was very confident in her sexuality. And she was curvy, like me.

Chrissy and Fiona cornered a newcomer to the house. The guy walked into the house with a cocksure grin. Now that he was surrounded by two beautiful, naked women writhing their bodies against his, he looked like a lamb that had stumbled into a lion's den.

They gyrated their bodies in time to the music while slowly undressing the poor boy. He offered no resistance. When he tried to give them a hand, one of the girls took his hands and occupied them with a part of her body.

A pair of hands came up behind me. I didn't startle. Everyone present knew that my body was off limits. I sank back into the warm spot that belonged to me and me alone.

Christopher wrapped his arms around my waist and then found my hands. He ran his fingers over the diamond on my left hand. "Having a good time, princess?"

"Hmmm," I nodded as he pressed a kiss into my temple.

"Hey, Crow," called a redhead dressed in pink lingerie that somehow worked for her.

"Hey, Priscilla. Long time, no see."

"You wanna play?" She peeled the top of her lingerie down to reveal freckled breasts.

Christopher grinned at her bare boobs apologetically. "Not tonight, Cilla."

That was always his response. *Not tonight.* Not, *no.* Not, *not ever.* I knew he hadn't closed the door on playing with other women some day, but neither did he seem to be in a rush to make that day happen anytime soon.

"Have you met my fiancée?" he asked.

Priscilla and I made polite small talk while she stood with her breasts exposed. When she and Christopher began talking motors, I excused myself. Christopher pulled me back for a kiss and a whispered *Love you* before letting me out of his hold.

I walked into the kitchen where Eagle pulled a tray of brownies from the oven. They were snatched up as soon as he set the hot tray down on the breakfast bar.

"Oh, look at that," said Eagle. "There's only one treat left. Who really wants it?"

A group of girls ponied up to the bar with eager grins on their faces. Eagle looked over at me.

"MK? You want in?"

"I'm good." I grabbed a seat at the dining room table. "I'll just watch."

The story is not over!

You know who's next!
Ready to watch Eagle soar into a relationship that
comes out of the blue?
Wait until you meet the one woman who might be
more than he can handle in
Slippery When Wet,
Book 4 in the Watchers Crew series.

Turn the page to see how it all goes down...

Chapter One

"NURSE CLEO, just what do you think you're doing?"

Dr. West's voice was shrill, like a varsity quarterback being stripped naked by the president of the geek club, then jeered at by the JV chess club, mocked by the extras in the theater club, and pointed at by the full cheer squad.

"I came in for a prostate exam," he said.

"Hmm," I purred, picking up the speculum and advancing towards him.

He lay back with his feet in stirrups, his knees up on an exam table. His bare ass cheeks clenched on my approach. My lips curled like a cat approaching a bowl of cream.

"So why are you giving me an anal exam?" he demanded.

I pulled on latex gloves, stretching the synthetic material down my fingers and then letting go of the end with a satisfying snap. West winced and my tummy tightened in anticipation. There was nothing in the world like watching a powerful man squirm as you slow marched toward him. Like a secretary who was smarter than her boss; like a wife who doctored the joint bank account; like a little girl wrapping her daddy around her pinky finger.

Dr. Simon West was the current big man on campus here at Sacred Heart Hospital. He had a string of letters after his name and a stack of medical journal articles by and about him. Everyone, including the Chief of Surgery, cowered in his wake.

Not me.

The bigger and louder they were, the wetter my panties got to bend them to their knees. In Dr. West's case, his knees were already bent. Bent back towards his belly with his ass presented in offering.

"I demand you let me up now, nurse." He spat the word *nurse* like it was an insult.

I gave his knees a shove, and they spread wider

without protest. The speculum slid easily into his ass. He tried to squirm away, but he didn't get far. He opened his mouth in what looked like an attempt at a scream, but it turned into a moan.

He liked it.

That wouldn't do. I cranked the device open. It turned the small opening of his anus into a large hole.

"Awww!"

There was the music my ears were waiting for.

"Dr. West," I said. "I'm checking your exit because you seem to have a problem putting your penis inside too many entrances."

West raised his ass as I gave the speculum one more crank. His erect penis lay shackled at his belly. The eye of his penis wept. The twin baby blues on his face watered as well.

"It's as I expected," I tsked. "These tests show that you suffer from chronic masturbation."

He squirmed on the exam table. In the stirrups used to examine women's cervixes, all ten of West's toes arched back towards his body. His ass was scooted down to the edge of the table. His thighs spread wide like a woman having her yearly pap.

"There's only one cure; we need to plug this hole." I gave the speculum in his ass another crank.

He gripped the table. His knuckles went white. His eyes glazed over in pleasure.

"There's nothing wrong with me." His voice was breathless, his chest heaved. "I demand you stop this now."

"I'm only trying to help you," I said.

"You're just a nurse," he panted. "You don't know what you're doing."

I snorted. "You surgeons all think you're God. The truth is that I save more lives in a week than you will ever save in your entire career. Whereas you couldn't find the scalpel without a nurse standing next to you. Isn't that right?"

I yanked the speculum from his hungry ass. He wailed in protest. His penis jerked inside its cage.

"What was that?" I said.

"Yes, Nurse Cleo." His blue eyes were glassy as he turned over his power to me.

The crotch of my blue scrubs went damp at the wild look in his eyes. It was a look of complete submission. My grin spread on the right side of my mouth, stretching East at the wickedness of it all. Now that I had his full attention, we could begin.

I cupped his balls in one hand and reached for the dildo with the other. Dr. West may have been a lion in the halls of the hospital, but I was about to turn him into a pussycat.

I held up the monster dick for him to see. His eyes widened, and he gulped. I wondered if he actually wanted me to do this? Not that it mattered. He was the type that would never safe word. He saw it as a sign of weakness. He was lucky I was a compassionate sadist.

I liked to make my subs suffer. But I also liked to play with them again and again. So, I tried not to break them. At least not irreparably. I oiled up the monster dick as Sacred Heart Hospital's heterosexual god panted in anticipation.

At some point in their lives, every man wants to be pegged. They're men, after all. They walk the earth pretending they have all the answers. But deep down inside, they're all little boys afraid of the awesome power that they wield between their legs.

It was a fantasy; a man that was actually in charge. Men could pretend all they wanted that they ruled the world. Most men walked a straight line. It was women that turned. Just like a boss, or a husband, or a clueless father, they all needed a woman's touch. It just so happened that I liked touching men's asses.

"Please," he whispered. "No."

West shook his head left to right. His thighs fell farther open as he held onto the idea that I was forcing him into this lewd act. As if I could force this six foot, two hundred twenty pound, testosterone-riddled man into anything. Not with all five foot four and one hundred sixty pounds of me.

Physically, I may have been your average woman. But my sexual proclivities were entirely, and wholly, and completely deviant. I shoved a bottle of lube up West's ass. His entire body shook and trembled at the invasion.

"Please hold your composure, Dr. West." I lined up the dildo with his hungry hole. "This is a necessary medical procedure. It should not arouse you."

As the dildo breached the first layer of his anus, he didn't tense. He completely relaxed under the assault. His eyes closed, and he had the look of a sub who was lost in a storm of pleasure.

The drip in my panties stopped. I knew I should have brought the thicker dildo. I'd already pegged him three times this week, and he'd adjusted. The good doctor was like an addict who'd tried weed on Monday and graduated to coke by Thursday.

I withdrew the fake dick. His eyes flew open like a newborn who'd heard a loud noise. His mouth formed a pouty O like he was about to let out a wailing cry. "What the fuck, Cleo?"

"What did you just call me?" I flicked at the pink cock cage that held his erection. His penis strained inside the metal bars.

"I mean, Mistress."

"Don't call me that either." I slapped his balls and his ass arched off the table. "You wish I was your Mistress. That's something you have to earn and you're not worthy. It's Nurse Cleo to you."

West's eyes were dilated. He was almost too far gone; lost in pleasure when I'd only given pain and frustration. Getting him off was too easy. I was getting bored.

Time to make this interesting. I slipped off my bottom scrubs and thong. West's eyes latched onto the key that dangled from my earlobe. It matched the lock to the cock ring he'd been wearing all day. I flicked my hair over my shoulder until it covered the ring. Some of the excitement left West's eyes.

I grinned as I climbed aboard the exam table. I hovered my bare pussy above his face. My knees boxed in his ears.

"Oh, thank you, Nurse Cleo." His grin returned. His tongue reached out.

I raised my hips. "Don't you dare touch my pussy. Lick my ass."

He did as he was told. He laved his tongue around the rim of my anus. I sat my cheeks down right on his nose.

"You are not worthy of this pussy," I said as I swiveled my hips all over his face, getting him covered in my scent. "But you want it, don't you?"

He couldn't respond with his tongue at work and his face covered. I knew it, but I didn't take it as an excuse. I slapped at his balls when I couldn't hear his response. The flesh of his straining penis was hot and throbbing in the tight cage. His moans of pain sent a thrill through my clit, which is why I didn't realize I'd gone too far until it was too late.

He wasn't allowed to come until I did. And he knew it. But, of course, the bastard shot off before I got there.

A cock cage strains the erection, not allowing it to reach its full potential. It makes coming difficult, but not impossible. West was an overachiever. I looked back as his cramped dick wept its pleasure.

"You greedy, little slut."

"Fuck," he sighed with a sated grin. His head lolled back as he continued to come down from that subspace high and noted the mess he'd made. "Aw," he chuckled. "I'm sorry, Cleo."

"What did you just call me?"

He blinked as though I'd awakened him from a wet dream. "Aren't we done? The scene, or whatever, is over."

He was done. I hadn't come yet. In fact, I hadn't come for weeks since I'd been playing around with him. The last time I came was the first time we'd fucked. The first time I'd broken him by sticking my fingers in his ass in the hospital supply closet.

That orgasm had been great. So great that I'd been chasing after it for the last two weeks. Tonight, just like the last half-dozen times I'd played with him; he'd gotten to the finish line before I'd gone a quarter mile. I prepared to climb off him and end things when there was a knock at the door.

"Dr. West?"

West looked pointedly at the straps on the stirrups. "Let me up, Cleo."

I stayed put, hovering my cunt over his face. A tingle zinged my clit as his eyes widened in true fear.

"Dr. West, are you in there?"

A wide grin spread across my face. "Do you want me to get that for you, Dr. West?" I asked, not quite loud enough to be heard outside the room.

"Yes," West called out to the door. "No," he whispered in a growl at me.

The door rattled. My mouth watered at the possibility of the intrusion. I wasn't an exhibitionist. I just liked the idea of West's terror at being caught in such a compromising position. But the pussy below me had locked the damn door. He was absolutely no fun.

"Can I come in?" said the person outside.

"No," said West. "I'm... tied up at the moment." He yanked at the restraints.

"You're needed in the ER," said the voice.

West's eyes lit. He wasn't only a sexual whore; he was also a surgery whore. "I'll be out in a minute."

He looked pointedly at me. I got up and untied him. I might play with him, but I didn't play when it came to my job. I pulled up my underwear and pants, tossed the latex gloves in the bin, and headed for the door.

"Wait," West called out behind me as he splashed water on his face. "Make sure the coast is clear."

"Yeah," I snorted. "Okay, Scooby."

I tossed up my thumbs and then reached out and turned the doorknob without looking first. If he wanted to hide his true nature, that was him. I didn't do closets.

CHAPTER Two

I LEFT the exam room and walked into a war zone. It wasn't a war zone like you'd find in the Middle East or Central Africa or even in Eastern Europe. There were no guns. No one wailed. No one was dressed in fatigues or cloth that covered them from head-to-toe.

There were a number of scantily clad girls in neon skirts and threadbare halter-tops. This city was a destination for randy Spring Breakers. So, my first thought was this was a backyard barbecue or beach bonfire gone wrong.

Then I noted that the few guys assembled were in jumpsuits that covered them from head-to-toe. There were smudges on everyone's faces, shoulders, hands and clothes. I wasn't a sports fan, but I knew racecar drivers wore flame retardant suits.

I entered the triage area and took stock. There were only four emergency room nurses on call at this time of day. It was lunchtime. A slow time in the ER. The most we got in at this time were work-related incidents; falls from changing light bulbs, ingesting ink through the mouth, ear, and eyes, even temporary blindness from copy machines.

I sifted through the scantily clad girls and sectioned them off to one side of the room. The major concerns in that mix were minor burns on their bare chests, scrapes on their knees, and soot in their weaves.

The men were a little worse-for-wear with burns on their hands. Some were coughing from possible smoke inhalation. Those I sent off with other nurses to check their ABC's; airway, breathing and circulation. The worst cases would need to be administered oxygen through a mask, but it was likely that most simply needed to breathe some clean air.

I approached a pale man with hair so light-blond it was white. He, too, was in one of the racing suits. There were burn marks along the fabric at his shoulder along with a patch of blood.

"Sir, let me have a look."

He jerked away from my touch like I was a hissing snake. "Don't touch me you fucking coon. You might give me an infection."

I didn't flinch at his diatribe. I'd been called

worse. He didn't hit on my least favorite slur; mutt. Because technically, that's what I was. I was a mix of just about every race from both of my mixed heritage parents, much like my namesake, Cleopatra.

I let him go. Misogynists turned me on because I liked breaking them. Racists made me want to trade my dildos for scalpels. Still, I had a duty to serve anyone who came through those doors.

"I told them to take me to Sisters of Mercy, the Catholic hospital," the racist said. "But they brought me to the fucking ghetto."

He stormed towards the ER doors, holding his shoulder. A small trail of males followed behind him. I caught a swastika on two of their jackets as they turned. Just before they headed out the glass doors of the ER, the doors slammed open and a gurney careened inside.

This blond male's eyes narrowed and his lips quirked. The guy on the gurney turned to him with a glare. The paramedics blocked them as they rushed patient inside. The paramedics began shouting out stats.

I took a look at the guy on the gurney. He was in one of the racing suits, but his suit was not wholly intact. Fire had made its way into the fabric at his shoulder and leg. His blond hair was pristine, but there were smudge marks on his face.

A girl raced to keep up with the gurney. Her short legs stumbling as they pumped alongside the big men to keep up. Tears streamed down her pretty face as she clasped the injured racer's hand. Her church girl ensemble seemed out of sorts with his devil-may-care looks.

"MK, babe, I promise I'm fine," the blond racecar driver said.

But he didn't sound fine. His voice croaked. He had to pause after every other word. He winced as she touched his shoulder.

I looked him up and down. There was blood on his costume, but I couldn't immediately determine the location of the wound. This case would be where the action was so I latched myself onto the gurney. I grabbed the chart and began the intake. Dr. West wasn't the only medical whore in the building.

"Name," I demanded.

"Crow." The racecar driver grinned at me.

"Real name?"

"His name is Christopher Trent," the church girl, MK, answered in his stead.

I addressed further questions about his identification to her. Once I got the age and details of the patient, I moved onto the important stuff. "Tell me what happened?"

"Car crash."

It wasn't the blond that answered. The voice rumbled on a low vibration that arrowed straight to my clit. The vibration was deep enough that it nearly finished the job that Dr. West hadn't been able to complete. I looked up, and then up some more, into a tall drink of whiskey.

His skin was like lava; the kind that oozes out of a molten chocolate cake. His lips were plump as though he'd been kissing someone very recently. His eyes were hard and intelligent.

"An accident?" I parroted.

Mr. Lava Cake exhaled quietly. "No."

His words were steady, but there was guilt rimmed at the edges of his eyes. My pencil stopped moving as I focused on him. I had the urge to heal that wound.

"You think they ran him into the wall on purpose?" MK's voice went shrill.

"Eagle." The blond patient glared at his dark-skinned friend. It was a warning.

The other man, Eagle, held Mr. Trent's glare, but Eagle didn't say anything further.

"Mr. Trent, tell me what happened?" I

addressed the blond, but my attention was focused on his friend.

"Please call me Crow," said the blond. "I didn't lose control." He tried to sit up, but when he did he winced in pain.

"Lie back," I ordered. "Stay still. You might have a concussion."

"He hit the guard wall really hard," said MK. Her voice was tinged with tears. "And then there was nothing but flames."

"I'm fine, I promise," said Crow.

But I could tell by the way he favored one side of his body that he wasn't. His friend, Eagle, must've seen the same.

"I need to know where it hurts," I said.

"I'm fine," said Crow. "I walked away from it. It was a bad wreck. But I got up and walked away. It's just some scrapes and bruises."

"How fast were you going?" I ignored his macho excuses and began examining him.

"Hundred and twenty," he grinned. "Had it for sure. Smoked them all. Until that idiot lost control of his stick."

"It's safe to say you have a concussion," I said peering into his eyes. "But there may be more going on. We need to wait for the doctor to examine you."

"You're not the doctor?" asked Eagle.

I looked over at him. "No, I'm a nurse. Nurse Cleo."

Even while his friend was in pain, Eagle was checking me out. I had the urge to preen, to lean over and show him how round my ass was. But I was a professional.

Dr. West came up to us. "I hear there was a racing accident." He grinned with eyes bright like a middle schooler arriving just in time to the schoolyard to watch a brawl.

"Mr. Trent was traveling at an excessive speed and hit a wall." I offered him the chart, but he ignored me.

"How fast?" West asked as he began his own exam.

I grit my teeth. I didn't know if West was intentionally trying to piss me off to get a punishment later, or ignorantly pissing me off to get a punishment later.

"I'm fine," Crow repeated. "It's probably just a concussion, like the nurse said."

"I notice that you're favoring one side and your breathing is labored," I said. "That could mean you have some trauma to your back."

MK trembled and squeaked. Crow glared at me

like he'd done with his friend. Like his friend, it had no effect on me.

"Back injuries are common in car accidents." I turned and addressed West. "So to be safe we should order some x-rays for his back, right Dr. West."

West made some notations on the chart. Then he turned to me without looking at me. "Nurse Cleo, it looks like we're good here. Why don't you get these pain prescriptions worked up for my patient?"

I raised an eyebrow at his tone. Standing next to me, I noted that Eagle did the same.

So, this was purposeful pissation. I had the urge to rattle the cage I had on his cock. Instead, I tried to communicate the world of hurt he would be in when I got him alone.

"Of course, Dr. West," I said as sweet as the asinine in me would muster. "Should I also add an MRI and X-ray for his neck?"

West smiled that fake smile; that condescending smile he gave to patients when he used big medical words. "Do you see that on the chart, Cleo?"

Visions of nipple clamps and ball weights danced in my head.

"Put it on the chart."

West and I both turned to the patient's friend.

Eagle's eyes were impassive, but his tone had been implacable.

"I don't see anything that indicates back trauma," said West. "It's probably a waste of money. I don't want you gentlemen to come too far out-of-pocket."

"Don't worry about my pocket," said Eagle. "Worry about my brother. Add the test."

Dr. West bristled at the command in that deep voice. His eyes lost focus for a second. Eagle plucked the chart out of my hand and handed it to West.

West shrugged as he took the clipboard. "It's your money." He made the notation, handed the chart to me, and walked away.

I turned back to the group. "Listen," I addressed Crow. "Do not get off this gurney. Lay back and relax."

"Yes, ma'am." Crow grinned.

I knew I needed to keep my eye on this one. He was trouble.

"He needs to rest." I addressed this to Eagle. "Don't let him move too much. He might feel fine but there could be something else under the surface. Maybe I'm wrong, but I'd rather be sure."

Eagle nodded. Our eyes connected. An understanding passed between us without words. I had a fleeting vision. What would that tall form look like on his knees? Would he come up to my belly button or the underside of my breasts? Would those dark eyes twinkle up at me as I buried his face between my thighs?

The corner of Eagle's mouth ticked up as though he'd read my mind. One eyebrow quirked up as though to say, *try it and see.* I walked passed him refusing to pick up the gauntlet he'd thrown down. I may fuck around with doctors, but I drew the line at patients and patients' sexy friends.

I had ethics; not many, but some.

CHAPTER Three

AFTER GETTING his x-rays and a few other tests done, I left Crow resting comfortably in his room with his eagle-eyed brother and his sweet, little girl-friend surrounding him. I walked down the halls to the nursing station.

Along the way, there were a few interns who leered at me. I stared back at them openly challenging them. I had no problem with my reputation at the hospital. West wasn't the first surgeon I'd bagged. Not by a long shot. And he wouldn't be the last.

Not a single one of the green interns interested me. I could break each and every one of them in a night. By morning, they'd be begging me to strap on a cock and shove it wherever I pleased. And, by the reddening of their baby cheeks, each of them knew it. Wanted it without knowing that it was a sexual option for them. But the glimpse at the forbidden made them gulp down that lump of sinful desire. It didn't take long for their eyes to drop along with their lascivious glances.

Yeah, thought so.

In the waiting room, I saw a number of other stragglers from the races. But one group stood out from the bunch. There were two guys there. One was big, like Hulk big. He was tall and dark and very handsome. The other was built like a gymnast; strong upper body and slim, muscular lower body.

Two women hung on the men. The foursome stood in a tight huddle with everyone's hands or shoulders brushing or embracing each one in turn. Unlike the other girls in the waiting room, these two women weren't scantily dressed. Also unlike the other girls who were draped haphazardly on the unengaged men hanging around, the Hulk and gymnast had their hands securely wrapped around the two girls.

It was clear that the foursome were two couples. But it looked like they were more. I knew the body language of lovers, and they were all very familiar with each other.

Swingers, maybe? The 70's fad was making a comeback with the Millennial generation. But instead of the term "swingers" the new breed of twenty-somethings called themselves Polys. I had no delusions about monogamy myself, but I was territorial with the things I considered mine.

The big guy caught my gaze. He took a few steps towards me. I actually considered taking a step back as his massive body blocked my path and my view. His voice was deep and gravelly like a bear who'd stolen a man's voice. "We're Crow's brothers."

He pointed between himself and the gymnast, who upon closer examination I saw was Asian to the Hulk's decidedly Spanish, or maybe Latino, features.

Brothers, he'd said? Definitely polyamorous.

"How's he doing?" asked Latin Hulk.

"He's resting comfortably right now," I assured him. "We're running some tests to be sure we know everything that's going on. We have to wait for the results to come back and then we'll know more."

"When can we see him?" This came from the blonde girl sandwiched between the two males. She looked as though she belonged in a church choir, and not the Southern Baptist kind of an urban community. No, she looked like she would sing hymns in a northern, Protestant church.

It was apparent the brothers of this racing crew had a type. The blonde church girl and the prim and proper brunette, MK, back in Crow's room. But the black woman, with a dangerously-short skirt and fuck-me heels that I had to get my own pair of, didn't quite fit the pattern. Still, she looked entirely comfortable and in place wrapped in the Asian man's arms.

"It'll take another sixty minutes for his tests to come back," I said. "You can go back there to his room. Just try not to get him excited. I need him to rest."

The group headed off. Arms around each other. They looked like a family. I stared after them, crossing my own arms over my chest. I felt a tug at my heart and scratched my chest. My eyes tightened as they turned a corner and went out of my line of sight. I turned away and made my way to the reception area where the other nurses were gathered.

"Cleo, can you sign Judith's card?" asked Midge, an older woman with gray streaked hair. Like most nurses present, Midge had been here for years. She'd gone to nursing school before I was born and had weathered Sacred Heart Hospital when it was a one-story charity hospital run by the church. The hospital had since gone public and taken in any soul regardless of what service they might need, be it contraceptive, sterilization, or abortion.

"I feel like I'm always signing these things," I said, taking the pen from Midge.

Judith, the previous Head Nurse, was retiring. She'd been at the post less than two years. The Head Nurse before that had only lasted nine months. Some were promoted, others moved to bigger hospitals with larger paychecks, and some left on maternity leave and never came back.

"I hope you're applying this time," said Midge. "You would be a shoe-in. You basically run this place anyway."

I shrugged instead of answering. But I knew she was right. Everyone knew she was right. After three years at the hospital, I had finally put my shoe in the ring for the promotion. But I had no intention of making it public yet.

I liked my current job. I didn't care to have any more responsibility than I already had. Being an ER nurse came with its own set of stressors. But my situation at home was getting more and more dire. I needed the money that came with the promotion, and this was the best way I knew to get it.

Still, administration was not my thing. I was a people person. I got off on bossing people around. And I could juggle a number of balls in the air at once. But I liked the freedom of checking out every once in a while. And I definitely didn't feel comfortable with people depending on me; which was ironic since I literally had lives in my hands on a daily basis. But those lives were in and out within a week or so. This would be permanent.

I clenched my fingers around the pen before letting it go. I brought that shaky hand to my forehead and felt a thin sheen of sweat. I took a deep breath and the feeling passed. I had to do this. It wasn't just about me any longer.

"Any messages?" I asked Midge. My voice was hushed as I asked.

She looked through the pile of sticky notes and shook her head.

I sighed with relief. It had been a rough week at home. No calls from home today didn't mean anything. I should probably check in. I reached for my cell phone but a loud snap jerked my head up to attention.

"Nurse."

The thing about nurses is we're not jumpy individuals. We don't startle easy from loud noises or fluids leaking out of various human orifices, or missing body parts. We lift our heads, assess the situation, and then we get to work.

So, when one of the new surgeons came to the nursing station, arms waving, face red, voice barking, we lifted our heads calmly.

He spoke with authority. But one look at his fresh white coat, clean scrubs, and pristine loafers didn't sway a single nurse. Not a single one of our scuffed shoes, or faded scrubs jumped at his command.

"I need a nurse," he demanded.

A few eyes found his. Eyebrows raised or eyes rolled. No patient was in danger of dying, we would know. We'd know it way before he did.

The baby doctor looked around the group like an indignant toddler whose mother gave him Cheerios instead of Fruity O's. I had a sudden urge to break him. I wanted to see what he'd be like when he whimpered and crawled when I wouldn't play with his little wee wee.

"I'll take care of it for you."

The voice didn't surprise any of the nurses. No one even bothered to turn to look at its owner.

Nurse Charity Clarke sauntered up to him in her size-too-small scrubs that gave a view to her cleavage.

"It's nice to know that some people around here are willing to do their jobs." The baby doctor waved his arm in front of Charity to precede him. Then he stared at the ass she suggestively wiggled as she walked in front of him.

"She gives all of us a bad name," said Midge.

"No," said another nurse. "That's Cleo. Her sleeping around with them like a cliché is what gives nurses a bad name."

I didn't take offense. Especially when it was said with a giggle. "Where else am I going to find a quality lay? I earned my reputation, and I'm not easy. Just ask Dr. Winkler or Dr. James or Dr. West."

The cackling and giggling that always accompanied my antics came to a dead stop, like the needle of a record player shoved to the side. All the nurses turned away, looking down at paperwork.

I felt the prickles at the nape of my neck. I knew West was standing right behind me. I plastered on a smile and turned around.

Sure enough, West stood behind me, glaring. "You're needed."

The command in his voice sent a thrill through me. I had no idea where his anger came from, but it enticed me to follow and see where it led. Hopefully, it would lead down to my sorely neglected clit.

"Yes, Dr. West."

I followed him, excited to free his cock from its cage and ride it. I was surprised he was ready for another round so soon. I followed him down the hall, but he didn't go into our normal restroom, or supply closet, or back stairwell. Instead, he went into my supervisor's office.

That fucking, weak pussy. He held the door open for me. I glared at him as I walked past.

CHAPTER FOUR

"COME ON IN, YOU TWO," said the hospital's Nursing Director, Wanda Steele. "Take a seat."

Wanda was at the same time a tolerant tyrant as she was a laid back micromanager. She'd back up any nurse who had a dispute brought against them by a patient or doctor. But behind closed doors, she'd read you the riot act if you crossed a line that was important to her.

Today, she looked weary around the edges of her eyes. Her usually perfect makeup needed another application. And her wig was slightly askew.

For anyone else, this might be a typical end-of-the-day weariness, but I knew Wanda too well. She was never weary. Unless she was coming down with something. I put a hand on the seat farthest from my boss, but I didn't sit.

"What's this about?" I asked standing my ground.

"Dr. West has filed a complaint about you," said Wanda, a sigh evident in her voice. "He says you countermanded him in front of a patient."

"Can he speak for himself?" I stared West down. He did not meet my eyes. "I made a suggestion based on the information I gained from the patient intake. Are you mad at me for having my patient's best interest in mind? Or are you mad because a patient's family member got in your face?"

Just the thought of that tall, dark and sexy mass

of yumminess making West grovel got me wet. I hadn't played a good game of cuckold in a long time. Eagle would be the perfect candidate for such an adventure. And West would make a great pawn to shove around the board.

"You act inappropriately around me. Sexually," West said. His lips pinched together like a baby with a soiled diaper.

"Do you really want to have a conversation about our sex life here?"

West flustered. He flung his arms out in my direction and turned to Wanda. "You see what I mean about how she's been sexually harassing me?"

"How am I sexually harassing the man I'm dating?"

West turned red. His fists balled. And I kid you not; he stomped his foot. "We are not. I've never taken you out."

"*Out* is not a part of my definition of dating. I'm not interested in watching you eat or hearing your opinion on a movie. We're fucking. That doesn't require going out anywhere." I cocked my head and reexamined him. "Unless there's some exhibitionist tendencies you haven't told me about?"

West turned to my superior and pointed his

shaking finger at me. "Do you see what I mean? I can't work like this."

Wanda looked between the two of us impassively. She rubbed at her temple with one hand and reached for a slip of paperwork with the other. "According to this, it appears that you two are dating."

"What is that?" West asked, lowering his finger and advancing to Wanda's desk.

"It's the report Nurse Williams filed with HR indicating that you two are seeing each other, and have been for the past three weeks." Wanda handed him the paperwork.

West jerked back as though the sheet of paper was poisonous. "I never filled that out."

"No, I did."

Whenever I was having a sexual relationship with a doctor in the hospital I always made certain to file with HR. Partially to protect myself in situations like these. But also to see them fluster when they got caught. I turned to West and his red face.

"Don't worry," I said, taking the paper from Wanda. "I'll rip that up. It's no longer needed since this relationship is now over."

West squirmed. I wasn't sure if it was because he didn't want our relationship to end? It didn't matter.

He no longer had a choice. He was a selfish lover. He'd given me the equivalent of blue balls twice now in one night. He'd already done the whole flustered at being caught thing that I so enjoyed watching. There wasn't any other way I could think to amuse myself with him. So, it was over.

""Would you excuse us, Dr. West," said Wanda. "I'd like a private word with Nurse Cleo."

West's indecision at the ripping of the paperwork dissolved. A smirk spread across his face as though he sensed he'd gotten me into trouble. I narrowed my eyes at him, and his lips twitched until the weight of my glare pulled the corners down into a cowing frown.

Yeah, it was so over between us. West shuffled out the door and I turned back to my supervisor. Wanda shook her head at me once we were alone.

I sat down in the chair, but scooted away from her as she pulled out a tissue and dabbed at her nose. "You coming down with something?"

"I'm fine," she waved my concern away. "You know you're a shoe in for this promotion, Cleo. But I can't promote you with your behavior. You have to set a good example socially as well as professionally."

"You know that's a double standard. Doctors

screw nurses all the time. You never see them getting called for their behavior."

"Because we're nurses. We have to set ourselves above those egomaniacs. You've been with us for three years. This is the first time you've applied for a promotion even though you would've been given the position years ago. What's going on? What's changed?"

I wasn't about to tell her the truth. I wasn't about to tell any one I worked with the truth. "I need a new challenge."

Wanda studied me, seeing right through me, but not the truth. "Fine. But you have to know that your reputation precedes you. If you really want this position, then you have to clean up your act with the doctors."

I shrugged. Doctors were just a pastime. They were an easy habit to break.

Inwardly, I smirked at my own joke. Outwardly, I nodded to Wanda. I couldn't afford to let this opportunity slip by me. Not with Toy getting worse and our time running out.

"I hear you," I said. "He's the last one. I promise."

"Cleo, I know how good you are, but if you want

this promotion you have to realize that the doctors also have a say."

"What? So they're gonna try and cockblock me? That's not fair. Any relationship I've had has been on file to avoid exactly this situation."

"It's still a boys' club, hon. Just stop fucking with them."

"Charity fucks with them."

"But she doesn't turn them into whining little girls." Wanda coughed and grabbed for another tissue.

"You should go home and get some rest."

She waved me, and whatever ailed her, away. I sighed and got up to head out the door. Of course West was waiting for me on the other side like the lap dog he truly was.

"What were you thinking filing a report with HR?" he demanded.

"What's the matter?" I smiled sweetly. "Were you embarrassed about our relationship?"

"What relationship? We were fucking."

I nodded patiently. "Those are the only kinds of relationships I have with men. Did you think it was something else?"

"You're a coldhearted bitch, you know that?"

My head cocked to the side, like the safety being

flung off a gun. My gaze narrowed at him, like I was looking at him down a barrel. "Call me a bitch again."

I watched him muster the courage. Then the bastard uttered the word.

I nodded slowly as I looked up and down his body for the perfect place to strike. My gaze latched onto his groin, and I grinned. I took the key from in my ear, the key that fit his cock ring, and placed it in my mouth. Knowing full well that I would regret this in a few hours, I swallowed. Luckily, I had no gag reflex. The piece of metal tumbled down my throat.

West gulped and then grabbed at his stomach as though he were about to vomit. "What did you...? How am I...?"

Exactly. It was gonna be a bitch on the way out, but damn it if it wasn't worth it for the look on his face.

"Kiss my ass," I said and turned on my heel. But I didn't get far. I walked into a mountain of hard muscle.

"Excuse me." The tall drink of water that called himself Eagle stood in my path. "We need a doctor"

"What's wrong?" both West and I asked.

Eagle ignored West and addressed me. "My

brother, he's losing feeling in his arm. He says not to worry about it, but I'm worried."

"It's probably nothing," said West.

"Or it's a spinal fracture," I said.

West turned to me. "Didn't we just have this conversation about you overstepping your bounds?"

I shut my mouth, which was hard for me to do. But I thought about that promotion.

"How do we know if it's a fracture?" Eagle asked.

"The x-rays," said West. "They should be back in thirty minutes."

"We need to put a rush on those," said Eagle.

"I can go and see," I said.

We headed down to the x-ray room. Eagle followed close behind. I felt him stalking behind me like a tiger. I knew his attention was on his friend, but my ass felt a hot gaze. When I chanced a glance over my shoulder, my suspicion was confirmed.

His lazy, hazel eyes were locked on the sway of my ass. He looked up and I was the one who felt like I'd been caught staring.

West opened the door to the x-ray room. He made to close it in my face, but I moved past him. Eagle did the same. West bit his lip and stayed mute.

In the room, two bodies were clasped together in

a corner. They sprang apart as we entered. I saw Nurse Charity's bare flesh from her rucked up scrubs, and I got a glimpse of what the new surgeon was working with. I felt a moment's pity that I wouldn't get to play with his toy.

"Excuse me, no patients in here," said the surgeon, his eyes looked past me and West to focus on Eagle.

Eagle glared. If it was possible, he seemed to grow larger in the small room while the new surgeon appeared to shrink. Eagle turned to me. He raised an eyebrow. Then he tilted his head. The silent command indicated that I should get to the business at hand; his friend's x-ray.

"Where's the tech?" I asked. "We need to rush an x-ray. It's an emergency."

"He went down the hall, but I can find it. Patient's name?" The surgeon was all profession-alism now.

I told him the name and he pulled the slides. He put them up in the light.

"Dr. Page," said West addressing the new surgeon. It was the first time he'd spoken in the ordeal. "Shouldn't we wait for the tech?"

"I can read an x-ray, West."

We all stared at it for a silent moment, but there

was tension in that moment. Namely from West and Page as they each raced to find any evidence in the film. West spoke first.

"Just as I said, there's nothing broken," said West.

"What about any fractures?" I asked.

"He wasn't exhibiting the signs," West insisted.

"Right here," said Page.

West grit his teeth as he glared at the back of Page's head.

"It's a hairline, but it's in the neck," said Page. "It could lead to a spinal problem. Has the patient experienced any numbing in the arms or dizziness?"

"Yes," Eagle spoke up. "He said his arm was feeling numb and he had a headache."

West peered closer. "It looks like he'll need immediate surgery. Let's get him prepped."

Eagle put a hand on West's chest. He didn't shove. He just stopped the man's motion. "Not you." He turned to Page. "You."

Doctors were a competitive bunch, surgery whores as I mentioned, so of course Page jumped at the chance to operate on any live body. "Nurse Charity, come with me."

"I want Nurse Cleo working with you," said Eagle.

Page looked over at me and shrugged. "The more the merrier."

We rushed out the room and down the hall to Crow's room. Page explained the procedure as Crow's brothers looked on with grim faces and each of the three girls' lips trembled.

As we were leaving the room with Crow on a gurney, Eagle made to follow. I pressed my hand against his chest. He was solid steel beneath my fingers. I felt his heart beating; fast and strong. Even though his face was stoic, it was crystal clear that he was worried about his brother.

"I'm sorry, you can't come," I said. "But I promise you, I'm going to take good care of your brother. I'll be by his side, watching over him every minute."

Eagle's large hand covered mine. I couldn't remember the last time a man had taken my hand in his own with or without my permission. It seemed like he held it there for an eternity, but I knew it was only a second.

He nodded and then stepped back and let me go. My legs took a moment to move. Then I disappeared into the surgery room.

CHAPTER FIVE

I WALKED out of the surgery room three hours later, which was five hours after my shift should have ended. In the waiting room, I saw that Eagle had Crow's girlfriend in his lap. MK's eyes were open but vacant. Eagle's hand stroked across her back where her bra strap would be.

The others were similarly seated together, holding one another close and offering support. This multihued, multiethnic group looked like a patchwork from afar. Up close, they made complete, harmonious sense. I wrapped my arms around myself, wishing I had a blanket to snuggle into.

As I came closer, Eagle's gaze connected with mine. His eyes widened and I saw fear and vulnerability glare through in his hazel depths. I held up my hand in a stop motion, trying to indicate that everything was okay.

His eyes closed for a second. His fingers tensed on MK's back. She didn't notice. I held up my thumb, pointing it towards the sky in the universal signal of *Everything's Okay*. His eyes closed again. In that moment I was free to look my fill of him.

I drank in the sight of him sitting there, vulnerable with another woman in his lap. I liked the picture very much. I wanted him on his knees, head tilted back at me, eyes closed, lips parted. Oh, the things I'd stick in that mouth.

Eagle's eyes flashed opened. They caught and held mine like he knew what I was thinking. Even though his eyes were open, I couldn't tell what he was thinking. I doubted this man had a submissive bone in his body. Unfortunately, that made me want him even more. It would likely take a lifetime to break him. But oh, during that time, I could make him hurt so good.

His eyebrow quirked in a challenge. I stuttered in my steps as I came to stand before him. My fight or flight response engaged. Something told me that another step forward would put me in a trap. A step backwards would get me chased. I wasn't a pussy and so I stepped forward.

The side of his mouth quirked up as I did. I couldn't tell what things he wanted to do to me, or wanted me to do to him. I couldn't read his kink, other than he was the type who liked to share. I knew he had to see that I wasn't the type of woman who was a toy. I was a toymaker.

He gave the woman in his lap a light tap. MK looked up. She blinked and slowly her gaze came into focus. She regarded Eagle, her eyes full of trust as she waited for further instructions from him.

That pulled me up short. I'd never had that; trust in a man. Or a woman for that matter. I didn't have some tragic childhood where a man abused me and that was why I liked to hurt them. I was an equal opportunity sadist. I spared the church girl's ass a moment of perusal as she stood to allow Eagle up, wondering what shade her skin would blush if handled correctly.

The other two men and their women stood as well. They all approached me as a unit. Each man and woman fanned out, surrounding me. The final formation wasn't a U shape that left me at the head. It was a circle, which included me.

"The surgery went well," I said. "He's resting comfortably."

A collective sigh of relief went through the group. MK's trembling hands were collected up by the Asian man. The blonde woman wrapped her arms around MK's torso lending further support.

I had given many families good news. I'd given my share of bad news, too. But I'd never felt included the way I did in the midst of this group. It left me with a sense of unease. I took a step back.

"The doctor will be out to tell you more, soon."

Before I could take another step in retreat, Eagle stopped me with a feather light touch on my elbow. "Will you tell us your prognosis?"

He didn't tug me. He barely had a hold on me. But somehow I found myself taking two steps forward and back into the circle of the group.

He released his hold on me and I was sorry for it. I liked this man more and more with each word he said to me. Visions of a gag shoved into his mouth danced through my mind.

"You were right to push for the x-rays," I said. "It was a fracture. If we had let it go, your brother could've had permanent spinal damage. You probably saved his life."

Eagle was silent. I could see his jaw working. The expression on his face reeked of guilt and shame. I wanted to take my words back, but I didn't know which ones had elicited that response. I'd hoped to make him feel prideful, vindicated.

"He's going to be fine," said the blonde girl who was wrapped around MK. She put her arms around Eagle and squeezed. He turned his head and kissed her temple absently, but his eyes remained on me.

I took a moment to take in the blonde again. She did not look like the type to be shared, but I knew from experience that it was usually the quiet girls that were the freaks. They were my favorite.

I liked my men to be assholes that I would break down into weepy little girls. I liked my women to be good girls that I could turn into kinky little toys at my beck and call. When the blonde's blue gaze met mine, I knew I could have her sucking my toes, my nipples, and then my clit in under an hour.

She jerked away from Eagle with a gasp and blinked at me. She knew it, too. The way she bit her lip told me I was probably wrong —it would likely only take ten minutes.

Beside her Eagle grinned, the shame and guilt dropped from his face and he let out a low chuckle as I sized up his companion and she lowered her gaze submissively.

"Good news, folks." Doctor Page's smug tone broke the spell. "Your buddy is going to be okay. As you know, I caught the fracture early enough in the x-rays and I was able to repair the damage. Mr. Trent will need to stay here and rest for a few days, but I expect a full recovery."

Everyone nodded at the doctor's words, but all eyes stayed on me. Each one of Crow's family members came up and thanked me, giving Page a cursory nod before turning to gather their things from the waiting room.

"I'm going to stay," said MK.

"I'm sorry," I said. "Only family can stay the night."

"They're engaged," said Eagle.

That surprised me. Most polyamorous groups I'd encountered didn't put any weight on legal partnerships.

"That counts," I said. "He's in post-op right now, but you can wait for him in his room, okay?"

"Thank you," she said.

She came up and embraced me. I felt her inhale and then slowly exhale. I rubbed her back. She gave me a brave smile as she let me go.

"Thank you," she repeated.

I nodded and turned on my heel. My legs were a bit shaky as I walked away. Again, I felt dark, smoldering eyes on my ass. But when I turned around, they were all gone.

I finally had a few minutes to myself. I clocked out before anyone could ask me to do anything else. I went into the locker room for my things. Checking my phone, I saw that there were no missed calls or messages. That was rare.

I swiped at my phone and dialed the contact

marked TOY. I tried not to get nervous when it rang the fourth and then fifth time. But on the sixth ring there was the clicking sound of a connection.

"Hello?" said a groggy voice.

"Hey, baby girl." I sighed with relief. "Did I wake you?"

I could hear her inhale, pushing the crust of sleep from her body. "You're still at work?"

"I'm leaving now. Just wanted to check on you. You had a good day?"

I heard her take another inhale. There was the creaking of a mattress as I assumed she tried to sit up in her bed. "There was a delivery guy. He knocked even though we signed that leave package form. I used the intercom and he left the package outside. I'm sorry, but it's still there."

"That's okay, baby. I'll get it on my way in."

"And there's a problem with the cable again."

"I'll schedule a tech to come out on my next day off."

"What time is it?"

It was seven in the morning, the start of a new day. Toy did well at night. It was the days that she often had trouble with.

"What happened?" she asked. "Why'd you stay so late? Was there some major accident the ER had to handle? Or did you get caught up under some doctor?"

"Both."

"Dr. Douche? Did he earn out of his chastity belt?"

I inhaled through my nose and scrubbed at my face.

"Uh oh, what did he do?" I could hear the laughter in her voice. It sounded good. This was my favorite version of Toy; happy and giggly. The anxious, fearful one was still asleep on the mattress.

"The idiot tried to tattle on me to my supervisor. So, I swallowed the key to his cock cage."

There was silence. And then Toy burst out laughing. "You're right, he is an idiot. I know better."

"Yes, you do."

"Because I'm a good girl."

"Yes, you are."

She purred into the phone like a kitten. I had the urge to race home and scratch behind her ears, rub her belly, and pet her in that special place.

"Anyway," I said as I closed my locker. "I'm done with doctors."

Toy laughed again. "You've said that before. And then a new jerk comes on the scene and you can't help but put his balls in a vise."

"I can't afford to anymore. We need the money."

She was silent for a moment. "It's my job to do the worrying in this relationship."

"It's my job to make things better so that you don't have to worry. That's what I'm doing now. Okay?"

"Yes, Mistress."

"Good girl. I'll be home soon. Do you need anything?"

"No, I put in an order with the grocery store and Amazon. Those should arrive this afternoon while you're home."

"All right. Then I want you to get up, take a shower, and wash that pretty kitty of yours."

"Yes, Mistress."

I caught the catch in her voice and it made me smile. "Good girl."

I got off with Toy. I wished I'd used my break to take a nap instead of play around with West, or Dr. Douche as Toy had so aptly labeled him. Instead, I was left frustrated and with a bout of indigestion. Still, it was a new day and I was making a fresh start.

Or so I thought, until I turned the corner and another cleansing product blocked my path.

CHAPTER Six

"THERE YOU ARE, NURSE CLEO."

"Actually, there I go, Dr. Page. I'm heading out."

"You did a great job in there," he said, ignoring my words. He rounded me, blocking my path, and leaned in.

People who were bigger than me always made the mistake of thinking that their size would intimidate me. I stared Page down with a glassy gaze, cold and unblinking. His confident smirk faltered. I raised an eyebrow and cocked my head, indicating that he should get down to business.

"I saw you've been having some trouble with Dr. West."

I sighed and rolled my eyes. I knew exactly where this little caring speech was headed.

Page cleared his throat and straightened his white coat. His eyes softened into predatory slits and his voice regained a false sense of confidence now that my glare was focused upwards.

"I have a solution," he said. "I think it would be mutually beneficial if we worked more closely together. I'd like to take you under my wing."

"I'm not interested in flying, thank you." Giving

him a curt smile that cut at the inside of my lips, I made to step around him.

Page blocked my path. Big mistake. But Wanda's words to play nice went through my ears. I rolled my neck. The cracking of the tendons in my neck worked to slow my mouth down from saying something stupid.

"You should consider it," Page said. "I know you're up for a promotion alongside Nurse Charity. The report I give could influence the decision depending on how well we work together."

I'd seen his work with Charity in the x-ray room. The next crack I heard were my knuckles. Luckily, I'd only balled my hand into a fist. It didn't connect with anything on his body —yet.

I looked Page up and down. It wasn't a long journey. It would be so easy to break this man. He had mama's boy written all over him. He was of that breed of Millennials that had everything handed to him. The kind of kid that was taught to the test and not to think for themselves. The kind of kid that had been praised for just participating in the game and given a trophy for showing up.

It would take me a day, two max, before I was in his ass with a monster cock and he was begging me for more. It would be so very easy.

I took a step back. "Dr. Page, both you and my supervisor will have to judge my work based on my merits. Between Nurse Charity and I, I'm sure the best woman will win."

Page looked up at the ceiling, as though he ran my words over in his head again and again. Then his jaw ticked when he realized he'd been rejected. "You've fucked every doctor in this place. You think you're too good for me?"

"Honey, I would be so bad for you." I reached out and patted him on his smooth, hairless chin. "I would turn you into my bitch and you would give me your job. But I don't have the time or the energy to play with you and work through your homoerotic tendencies right now. I need to get home."

"Oh yeah." He tilted his baby chin up and down. "I heard you were a lesbian."

"Sure," I said. "If that makes you feel better."

"Cleo?"

I caught sight of Wanda in the distance. Dr. Page took two steps to the side of me as she came to join us.

"You're supposed to be long gone," said Wanda.

I wanted to say the same to her. Her nose was red and her eyes puffy. I knew that if I fussed, she'd brush my concern away. From years of nursing I could tell that whatever had taken a shot at her would knock her down soon enough.

"Mrs. Steele, I'm glad you're here," said Page. "I just wanted to tell you what a valuable asset I think Nurse Charity is. Her help was instrumental on the surgical floor today. Not only that, but she caught a mistake another doctor had made."

Wanda looked to me. "Is that so?"

I remained mute. I was too tired to play this game. "I'll see you both tomorrow."

"Cleo," called Wanda. "Are you on the schedule later tonight?"

"No, I'm off. I'm going to spend the day with my girlfriend. We've got some lesbian stuff to do."

I rounded the corner, thinking I'd escaped any more roadblocks when I walked into a wall of a chest. What the hell? Was I a magnet for man boob today?

There was no flab on this chest. It was all muscle and sinew and sin. Eagle reached out and steadied me. I took a step back and met the wall. I didn't like men caging me in. I always had the upper hand. I resented that I had to look up so far. I'd felled men taller and broader than him. But there was something about the rock hard presence of him that seemed impenetrable. Damn, I wanted to climb that wall.

Eagle stepped back and gave me room to breathe. "You headed out?"

"Yeah, my shift is over. Was over before your friend's surgery. But..."

"Thank you for that."

"You don't have to thank me. It's my job."

"Don't do that." He gave a forceful shake of his head to accompany his directive. The command in his voice called me up short. "You and I both know who did their job today."

I didn't answer. He didn't need me to. A man like him didn't need to see any recommendations or reports. He'd likely looked at me while I was doing his brother's intake and made up his mind.

"Can I ride down the elevator with you?" he asked.

"I'm taking the stairs."

He held out his hand for me to precede him. I headed into the stairwell.

"I owe you," he said as the door shut behind us.

"No, you don't," I said, bracing my hand on the rail to steady myself. "The hospital pays my bills."

"I wasn't offering cash."

I turned and caught those hazel eyes. I knew exactly what he was offering before he spat out the words. My steps halted, but I kept my grip on the railing.

"So, is there anything else you might need?" he asked.

His voice was a purr. There was a gulf of space between us, but I felt like those words reached out and pinched my tits. I pressed my thighs together.

"Anything at all you might need?" He was beside me, but he took a step down below me, so that he had to peer up into my face.

His head tilted back. His lips parted. There was a hint of vulnerability on his face, just a hint. He let me look. Fuck if I didn't want to wrench his head back and expose his Adam's apple.

My panties dampened as I looked down at him in the submissive pose he'd struck. He inhaled as though he knew my juices scented the air, the bastard.

"Just ask," he said. "And I'll give it to you."

How did he know I needed to come so bad? I'd been denied by Doctor Douche earlier. I hadn't had a good orgasm in days. I couldn't remember the last time a guy had worked me over enough to elicit something from my pussy, but I knew this guy could. If I let him.

"It looks like you need something," he said, "and I'd really like to give it to you."

A door above us opened and voices poured down. It broke the trance. Thank god.

"Too many people use this stairwell." That was not what I meant to say. I'd meant to deny him out right.

"We can go somewhere else."

I shook my head. "An orgasm is not on the invoice."

"It would just be between us."

I shook my head, slowly, left to right. I swore I heard it creak against the pressure. "I'm taking a break from men."

He grinned sadly, taking another step down, putting himself in an even more submissive stance. Did he know what he was doing to me?

"As you wish," he said. He stepped back into the railing, giving me a wide berth to pass.

It took a few seconds for my legs to work. I gripped the railing on both sides as I made my way down. He followed at a respectable distance.

"You guys are race car drivers?" I tried to change the subject.

"Yeah."

We reached the ground floor and stepped out

into the sunlight. "What happened on the track? You don't seem to think it was an accident."

Eagle turned his face into the sun. I didn't think he was going to answer. We were at my car by the time he spoke.

"It was a bump and run," he said.

"That sounds kinky."

He gave me a half smile, but his eyes were still far away, probably back at the racetrack. "It's when a car that's behind you taps your bumper. It makes you slow down and then the other car can speed past you."

"Sounds like cheating to me."

He nodded. "Yeah."

"Did the other driver get hurt?"

He nodded again. "Minor wound. He went to a different hospital."

I remembered the blond haired racist and his merry band of Nazis that had stormed out of the ER as Crow was being brought in. "Are you guys pressing charges?"

"The track officials are investigating it now. What will most likely happen is he'll be slapped with a fine and have to sit out one or two races."

Something in the tense set of his jaw told me that that wouldn't be the end of it. I just hoped that whatever he, and the rest of his brothers, were planning didn't end him up in my ER again.

"Your brother is going to be okay," I said.

"Thanks to you." He gave me a soft smile. Any thoughts of violence wiped clean from his handsome face.

"Thanks for walking me to my car." I unlocked the door and slid into the driver's seat. He shut it for me and leaned against the frame as I turned over the ignition.

The car wheezed. I tried again. It coughed. The last thing I needed was a car repair bill on top of the other crushing debt that Toy and I were under.

I jumped at the knock on the window. Eagle smiled and made a motion for me to roll the window down. I did.

"I can fix that, too," he said once there was no longer glass between us.

My hand turned the ignition again. This time the engine kicked over. I grinned triumphantly at Eagle. His smile was filled with patience.

"You let me know when you change your mind, Nurse Cleo."

"*When* I change my mind?"

His answer was a patient smile that touched his eyes, accenting his flaring nostrils.

In response to that carnal invitation, I flipped him the bird.

"Please," he said.

My finger wobbled. I was a sucker for making a grown man beg. He chuckled like he knew my kink and was playing with me. I rolled up the window and took off. That guy was dangerous. I pressed the gas and put as much distance between us as fast as I could.

Are you ready for this epic battle of two Dominants? Neither is going down without a fight. There will be orgasms... many, many, many orgasms.

Start Eagle and Cleo's story now!
Read *Slippery When Wet, Book 4 in the Watchers Crew series*

SLIPPERY WHEN WET **is the fourth book in the Watchers Crew series; a scorching hot, urban erotic romance series that explores themes of domination, menage, and open relationships.**

If you like your heroes alpha and multiple, then you'll love the men of the Watchers Crew.

Buy *Slippery When Wet* today and explore a world where there's always a happy ending, but it's shared.

Lover of fairytales, folklore, and mythology, Ines Johnson spends her days reimagining the stories of old in a modern world. She writes books where damsels cause the distress, princesses wield swords, and moms save the world.

You can sign up for her mailing list and receive alerts and free reads at http://bit.ly/InesReaders.

The Watchers Crew

Test Drive

Cruise Control

Dangerous Curves Ahead

Slippery When Wet

Smart Baztard

a free story in the world of the Watchers Crew available exclusively to

Ines Johnson's Readers Group.

www.ingramcontent.com/pod-product-compliance
Lightning Source LLC
Chambersburg PA
CBHW070830190726
48292CB00006B/2167